Covering the Cowboy
COWBOY WANTED
BOOK THREE

BA TORTUGA

Covering The Cowboy

Copyright © 2024 BA Tortuga

Cover Art Illustration by Alexandria Corza. Used with permission.

Editing by Sue Meadows

This is a work of fiction. Any resemblance to any person, living or dead, is purely coincidental.

All rights reserved. No part of this eBook may be used or reproduced in any manner whatsoever without written permission except in case of brief quotations embodied in critical articles or reviews. For information electronic address Turtlehat Creatives help@turtlehatcreatives.com

1st Edition Turtlehat Creatives 2024

Chapter One

"Wait, did I hear you correctly?" Tom tilted his head, trying his damnedest to parse what the drawl on the other end of the phone line could be saying.

Tom's little side hustle website was becoming quite a business, and he knew it. Cowboy Wanted was very popular—both on the side of the folks wanting help and the cowboys hunting work.

He got help for ranchers. He found drovers for gentleman farmers. He hired cowboys for bailing hay and rounding up horses.

He had a contact with a passion for helping wild mustangs. He had a section in the ads for handyman work and babysitting.

He'd even managed to get someone a date who saved a crumbling marriage.

But this was new.

"You wanna take naked pictures of a cowboy?"

"What?" That was pure-D shock. "No, not naked —kind of shirtless maybe. You see, I write romance novels. In fact I write gay romance novels, and I need a cover model. Everybody's used everybody. I feel like there's no new faces in the world. And we don't, you know, we don't even have to show faces. It can just be like a chin and down. But I need somebody with a decent belly. I need somebody who can wear a pair of Wranglers who seems like he was actually meant to wear them. I don't need some sort of a bulked-up bodybuilder. I really need a nice-looking man, possibly with a tan and a six-pack, who can wear a cowboy hat and has great hands. You know, that's the big thing I need. Great hands. Great hands on a belly. Great hands on a belt buckle. Great hands shoved into a pocket of their jeans. I need great hands."

Wow. Okay. So, writers obviously were chatty. Cool.

"Do you have a photographer?" This was the weirdest thing he'd ever heard of, but cool.

He was totally not the right type, but he would totally be willing to get naked and stand for a photographer. Koby would love that.

"Of course I have a photographer. She's having trouble finding the right cover model, and I happened to come across your site. I'm local, you see, and I thought I'd give it a try. I'm sorry, I didn't mean to waste your time."

"No, no, no, Mr.—"

"Williams. My name is Austin Williams."

Tom hooted. "That is a kick-ass name."

"Thanks, I use it for my books too. I—yeah…"

"So, Mr. Williams, you didn't waste my time. I can do it." He wasn't really sure how he could do it, but God knew he could do it. It might require a spray tan, but he could do it.

"Call me Austin. And you think so? It would save my life. I've got a whole series that I'm recovering, and we're going to put them out. I'm trying to relaunch before my new series starts, and I just—I think I can make it work. I have money in the budget for the photographer and model fees."

Lord have mercy. "Well, okay. Let's make this happen. So how does this work exactly? I've never done this."

"I'm not the professional, but I can e-mail you my photographer's information, and she'll be able to talk to you about cover model releases. And, you know, locations and all of that stuff. I don't even have to ever meet the guy. It's not skeezy, and it's a no-contact thing. I'm trying to help the photographer and myself out. I'd love to have a cover model who's mine, exclusive."

Okay, dude. Breathe. "Fair enough. I mean, seriously. I can do this."

"If you can do this, it would really make my year, man. I appreciate it. I'll e-mail you all the contact info, budget, everything like that."

They finally said their goodbyes, and Tom hung up the phone and started thinking hard. Who did he know who was sexy?

Someone who wasn't his lover, because he didn't want his husband on the cover of sexy books. He wanted his husband to himself.

Whoa. That sounded like an awful possessive thought. Tom grinned feeling a little like the Cheshire cat. He'd have to go tell Kody. It would so turn him on.

Then they could figure out who the second hottest cowboy was in Aspen and start from there.

Chapter Two

Kyler Hale needed a side hustle.

He had land. He had the money to build a house. What he didn't have was the money to pay the rent in Aspen while he waited for the house to be built.

He couldn't simply live in a horse trailer on the property these days. That might have worked when he was on his own, but he had Paige now, and while she'd lived with him in said trailer and in hotels on the road for her first years, she was fixing to start school.

"Daddy! I want to wear my boots tomorrow."

"Hmm?" He glanced up from the site he was scrolling through. It was called *Cowboy Wanted*, which seemed like it had to be a joke, but it was legit, according to the Better Business thing and the Chamber of Commerce.

"My boots. I need you to help me polish them."

"Okay, baby girl. I'll buff them up for you." He clicked the call me form thingy. "You got your outfit all picked out?"

They'd met Paige's teacher, even though they'd registered late enough that they missed the big welcome meetup. Now she just had to show up on time for her first day.

Not easy for a kid who'd done preschool with a bunch of barrel racer moms and roughstock riders' wives as teachers.

"Uh-huh. My pink Panhandle shirt with the fringe and my silver belt buckle."

"Smart choices." He wondered how long it would take for someone to tell her it wasn't Halloween. But his girl was a cowgirl, and she wasn't going to change that for any fancy new school.

"Do you think they'll like me?"

"Of course they'll like you. You're amazing." Why wouldn't they like her? She was down-to-earth, friendly, cute as a button, one hell of a rider, and a not half bad roper for being five.

"Right. And pretty soon we're going to have horses and cows and goats and chickens and ducks and llamas and buffalo and zebras and ostriches." She spun in a circle.

Oh, for fuck's sake. "Breathe, girlfriend. Let's start with horses. Maybe a couple cattle."

"And chickens, Daddy, you promised chickens."

Note to self—do not promise anything involving buffalo, zebra, or those fucking mean dinosaur birds. "All right, we can have some chickens, but you have to take care of them."

"Okay. I want to name them." Completely unafraid, completely unconcerned—this was a child who had grown up around animals and rodeo cowboys—who were basically animals.

She was going to eat the other kindergartners alive.

"Should I wear my hair down, or should I have it in braids?"

"I think you should have it however you feel like on the day, my love."

Her thick blonde hair was going to be the envy of all the girls when she got to be a teenager, but right now? Just trying to tame it was about all he could do. Thank goodness he'd learned to braid, and Henley was one hell of a teacher.

Hell, Henley was one hell of a mom. The problem was she was a better barrel racer, and she couldn't settle down with a little girl in tow.

Kyler got it. It wasn't like they were some big love match. They were two people who had hooked up because they didn't have anything better to do, and folks were starting to wonder.

Of course, then they had somehow caught pregnant.

That had been the best thing that ever happened to him. His Paige was the light of his life. She was the light of Henley's life, too.

It was just that it was hard to see that light past all the glitter and sequins.

And he had to be honest. Her rodeo career was going to last for decades longer than his possibly could. Saddle bronc riders had fairly short expiration dates.

So Henley took Paige whenever she could. She had a tiny condo in Dallas, she was always welcome to stay with them when she was in the area, and she called Paige every single day to see how she was doing.

"Yeah. I'll decide the night before, because if you're going to do braids I have to get up fifteen minutes earlier because it takes you forever…" Her tease was so familiar.

"I will beat you, girl," he mock-growled, making her giggle.

"I'm so scared, Daddy." She rolled her eyes and grinned at him, then came over for a hard hug. "They are going to love me at school."

Good Lord and butter, she seemed just like her momma when she said stuff like that, and he was scared for those kids.

Because they better like her or she was gonna eat them like he thought. His girl was a cowgirl through and through.

His phone chimed, and he checked it even though it

wasn't Henley's text tone, which was the stabbing sound effect from *Psycho*...

It was an e-mail from Cowboy Wanted.

Thank you for your interest in Cowboy Wanted. I've sent you a QR code to the forms I'd like you to fill out for the necessary work information and background check. There's also a place for you to upload a few pictures if that works for you. Once I have the relevant information in hand, I'll be happy to contact you for an interview.

Thanks!

Thomas Foster, Owner, Cowboy Wanted

"Is everything okay, Daddy?"

"Yep. I'm hunting around to get a little bit of extra work while you're in school to help build the house." He'd learned to never lie to her but to always put things in the simplest terms.

"Ew. Can I go watch *The British Baking Show Junior*?"

"Sure, kiddo. I'll be there in a few." He did love to watch kids bake. It made him smile.

"Okay." She skipped off.

He shrugged.

What the hell. He might as well fill out the forms.

What could it possibly hurt?

Chapter Three

Austin parked the Acadia, closed his eyes, and counted to ten.

Then he counted to ten again.

Then he counted to ten one more time. All right.

He wasn't sure why the school had called him again about Dallas.

But he knew what it couldn't be.

He knew his son hadn't gotten into a schoolyard fight. He knew the chance of his son having gotten hurt playing on any playground equipment was as likely as a hurricane in Nebraska. His son was not apt to talk back. He wasn't into talking at school at all.

So this was either some asshole kid had beaten his son up again. Maybe Dallas had had an asthma attack in PE class. Or possibly he'd simply refused to answer when the teacher called on him.

Maybe Austin should homeschool.

He really didn't have time to homeschool.

He had books to write, and it was tough as hell to write

books while homeschooling your awkward yet brilliant six-year-old.

God, how had he ended up with a six-year-old? Seemed like yesterday he'd picked Dallas up from the hospital, the surrogate having already left after her delivery. Dallas had been such a tiny little thing. So frail and riddled with lung problems, even then it hadn't mattered.

Not for a single second.

Austin had fallen in love at first sight, and that hadn't changed.

However, all the love in the world didn't make him want to homeschool.

He got out of the car, straightened his T-shirt and headed across the still-warm parking lot as if he were storming a castle.

Austin waited at the door of the school to be allowed in. And then he wandered in toward the office with a patently false smile on his face.

"Mr. Williams. Please come in. Principal Waters will see you in just a few minutes."

He gave Kari Ann, who was sitting behind the desk, a conspiratorial grin. "So what happened?"

"Well...we're waiting for another parent."

"So did somebody hit him? Push him? Is he okay?" Jesus, he'd wanted to have a charismatic, popular kid who was invited to every party.

He'd ended up with a little geek, like him.

Seriously, he knew why he was sort of that guy. He hadn't been tough and outgoing, but then he had a brother and sisters, not to mention his mom and dad with these huge personalities.

So even if he hadn't been the most sociable, socially acceptable kid on Earth, nobody had noticed. He was just one in the sea of Williamses.

And he'd always had a book. That was something else he and Dallas had in common.

Her smile widened. "He's perfectly fine. Seriously? You're never going to believe this one."

"Uh-oh." Okay, curiosity was going to kill him. He was a writer. He could come up with half a dozen impossible scenarios without even breathing hard...

"Yeah, a little oh, but mostly aww." She grinned at him. "Just remember that you still love him."

"Right. Now I'm really scared."

"Please, have a seat."

He tapped his Birks on the floor, amusing himself with possibilities while he waited.

Maybe Dallas had been abducted by aliens.

Maybe Dallas had won the Nobel Peace Prize.

Maybe Dallas had developed amazing superpowers—invisibility, super strength, the ability to shoot anti-bully rays from his eyes...

About the time he'd convinced himself that Dallas was going to be overlord of the universe, a tall son of a bitch walked in, wearing dirty jeans, a button-down shirt that had seen better days, and a cowboy hat that had been beat to hell and shadowed his face.

Lord, it was like Pig Pen. He walked right up to Kari Ann and said, "Pardon me, ma'am. The rumor is that you have my little girl here in the principal's office."

Kari Ann just smiled. "Hello, Mr. Hale. Yes. Have a seat. We're waiting on another parent."

Austin blinked at this Mr. Hale. Then up at Kari Ann "What? They ganged up on him? You telling me there was more than one? This is kindergarten. How is this fair or reasonable?"

"I guarantee you my little girl didn't gang up on anybody!" Pig Pen snapped, and Austin gave him his best eyebrow, while still glaring at Kari Ann.

Kari Ann opened her mouth to answer, when a woman in a suit and heels so high she had to be begging to get an ankle broke stormed through the door.

Ah, Elizabeth Franklin. Lawyer, head of her HOA, and mother to Wayne Franklin, the little shit who had broken Dallas's glasses twice.

Her ever so carefully coifed hair reminded him of growing up in Texas, the mass of highlights not even moving a bit in the breeze. He couldn't imagine how much superglue it took to stick hair on a head like that, but it had to take quite a bit.

"You get me Charlene Waters, and you get her for me right now!" Franklin said. "I will not have anyone accusing my son of bullying someone."

She met Austin's eyes, and pointed one finger at him and man, that fingernail was long and sharp. Good thing he knew they ended up being dull for the most part, those acrylics. His mom wore them all the time. "This is your fault. Your son is a sniveling crybaby and possibly needs to be in a Special Ed class. There's something not right about him."

Pure ice hit Austin's veins like he'd been dunked, and he stood up.

And up.

And up.

There wasn't a whole lot about him that was intimidating, but being six-six didn't hurt a God damn thing. "Pardon me? Am I to assume that your son is one of the troglodytes terrorizing mine? Again?"

"'Troglodyte'?" she screeched.

"Yes, dear. Troglodyte. You know. Cave dweller? Comes from the Greek root *trōglē*, which means hole or cave. The adjectival form is troglodytic, and somehow I don't have the slightest doubt you understand what it's like to be a wee bit troglodytic yourself. You know, a hole?" He let those words come out in his very, very best sneer.

Rule number one. Never fuck with an author. Rule number two. Never fuck with an author's child. These were rules to live by. Austin was convinced of it.

The cowboy chuckled, soft and low, and he glared over, but he just got a bland smile.

"Ah, looks like we're all here." The principal came out of her office. "Please join me, all of you. Thank you, Kari Ann."

They followed her, Franklin marching, him and the cowboy sauntering.

"Please sit down," Principal Waters said.

"Daddy! Daddy, the boy was being mean to Dallas. He pushed him down, stole his glasses, and he was going to poop on him. He said so. And so I kicked his butt, and I'm not sorry." That little girl's eyes were lit up with pure fury, her shirt was ripped, and one of her braids was all askew.

He searched out his son who was sitting next to the girl, one eye blackened, glasses gone, and that rage hit him again. "Seriously?"

The man sitting beside him muttered, "How troglodytic."

"What nonsense. You know full well that my Wayne wouldn't do anything like this."

"'m not a liar. I do not lie. That Wayne is a bully. He pushed Dallas down. He shoved him onto the ground. He took his glasses, and he has them in his backpack. And then he said if Dallas told he was going to squat down and poop in his mouth. I don't lie."

"Well, that's just nonsense. He wouldn't."

Austin arched an eyebrow at Dallas. "Son? Is your friend there telling the truth?"

Dallas nodded without saying a word.

"I waited until you got here to do the backpack search,"

Principal Waters said. "And I had Miss Grange here watch them while I came to get you so no one could cry foul play."

"So, do it. Dallas needs his glasses."

"You do not have my permission to search it," Franklin stated.

"I don't need it. There's a definite reason to suspect, and I am only searching for the glasses in his backpack."

"My girl doesn't lie, lady," Cowboy Hale drawled. "They'll be in there, and if they are, your son is all the bad things they say and more." He gave her a pointed glare. "I can see where he gets it from."

Oh, nice one. He fought the urge to fist-bump the guy. That would be frowned on, Austin thought. But if that guy's kid had defended Dallas, he was grateful.

"And who, exactly, do you think you are?"

"That is my daddy, Kyler Justin Hale, the bronc rider." That little girl was a firecracker. "Don't you be mean to him!"

The lawyer's lip curled. "Or what?"

"Mrs. Franklin, that's quite enough." Principal Waters' voice was cold as ice. "Paige, please sit down. Wayne, your backpack. Now."

If he was straight, he'd so be into her.

The glasses were in there. Broken again, of course, but in the backpack.

"I bet they were planted."

The principal, the cowboy, and Austin stared at her. "Come again?" Austin spat.

"One of them planted them so they could get Wayne in trouble, and then she probably hit him so that there would be bruises."

"I did not! You liar!" Paige stood, face screwed up, and her daddy shook his head, raised one hand.

"You know full well that that's not what happened."

"Nonsense, Wayne is..."

"This is enough," Austin snapped. "I want to press charges."

"What?" The shock in Mrs. Franklin's voice was delicious.

"This is the third pair of glasses. He's going to have to go to the doctor for that eye. I want to press charges, and I want Wayne out of my son's class. Immediately."

"I'll call the police, then."

"You will not. I'll sue you."

"For?" He couldn't wait to hear this one.

"For— for harassment."

That was weak, and they both knew it.

"You will not. It's well-documented that your child is a terrorist."

Wayne, who had been oddly silent, grunted, wrapping his arms around his waist. And Austin would have felt bad for him, but he'd had ample opportunity to amend his behavior already in this very short school year.

And he hadn't.

"I'm taking Wayne out of this shitty school." Franklin slapped her hand down on the principal's desk.

"That doesn't change the fact that Mr. Williams wishes to have the police called." She hit the intercom button on her desk. "Kari, Mr. Williams would like to press charges." She was cool as a cucumber.

"Yes, ma'am."

"Now, if you would like to go sit in another room with a teacher present while we wait, you're welcome to," Waters told Franklin.

"I want to talk to my son."

"Naturally. Miss Grange, take them to the lounge? I believe Mr. Diaz is in there."

"Yes, ma'am."

Once they were gone, the principal turned to him and Hale. "I'm very sorry about all this. Would you like Paige and

Dallas to go out and wait with Kari Ann while we discuss things?"

Kari Ann appeared at the door. "I made the call. Paige, Dallas, would you like some juice and a cookie?"

"I love juice." The girl jumped to her feet, holding out a hand for Dallas. "Come on, Dal. We'll go have something yummy and let the adults do adulty."

Dallas glanced at him, and he nodded. "Sure, son. Go have a cookie. I'll be out in a few."

"Okay, Poppy." Dallas slid off his chair and followed Kari Ann and the little girl out of the office.

"So." The cowboy leaned back in his chair and crossed his feet at the ankles. "Can you tell me exactly what happened?"

"Of course." Principal Waters sighed. "Wayne is a bully. It's a situation we've been dealing with since the start of the school year. As you can see, his mother is not at all helpful. His father is... distant. He travels for work."

"And this is the third time he's attacked my son," Austin snapped.

"Yes. We had already set the wheels in motion to switch Wayne's class, but frankly, we're a small school with right over four hundred students. We don't have that many classes." She folded her hands. "Wayne has already been in detention, so our next course of action is suspension. Which, if you press charges, Mr. Williams, will be the only option."

He stared at her. "Am I supposed to feel bad for him?" His kid was sporting a black eye.

"No, of course not. I simply wanted to apprise you of the situation." She switched her gaze to Hale. "Now, as for Paige, what she did was completely understandable. In fact, we encourage students to step forward if they witness bullying behavior."

Hale grinned a bit. "Well, that's sure what she's been taught."

Williams smiled faintly in response. "Yes. But we also suggest that, if the behavior persists, that students go and get the closest adult rather than taking matters into their own hands."

"Uh-huh." Hale crossed his arms now too. "You telling me my kid is going to get detention?"

"No, sir. But I will have to file an incident report."

"You gotta be kidding."

"It's protocol."

"Look, I want to file a police report, even if I don't actually get any action on this. But I do want him moved out of my son's class sooner rather than later. Agreed?" Austin was really starting to get peeved.

"Yes." Principal Waters nodded. She recounted the incident as she filled out the forms. Wayne had accosted Dallas. Threatened to shit on him. Paige cleaned his clock. And then a teacher had stepped in.

She handed them the report to review just as the police showed up.

When Hale stood and took off his hat for the officers, Austin stared.

Oh.

Oh no fucking way.

He knew that cowboy. Sort of intimately.

Kyler Hale was on the cover of his best-selling series...

Chapter Four

When it was all said and done, it was damn near time for school to be out, the cops had left, and Kyler was in a shit mood.

Paige hadn't done a thing wrong, but she'd gotten written up anyway. And that poor kid with the black eye...

He walked outside with the kids and the other dad, peering at the sky, which was clouding up. "You gonna take him in to urgent care?" he asked.

"No. I'll take him to his regular doctor tomorrow. She always has a few appointments to squeeze people into just for things like this."

He grinned at Paige, who was still holding the little boy's hand. "Y'all want to go to lunch?" Kyler wasn't sure why the hell he'd asked that, but he wasn't going to take it back. Paige's face lit up like Christmas, dammit, and he thought she'd found a fast friend.

"You want to, Dal? You didn't get to eat your sammich. We can both get something different and share!"

"Can we, Pop? Please?" the boy asked. "Paige is my best friend. She can ride horses, and she wants to play T-ball."

The other dad inhaled, then smiled. "Yeah? T-ball is great."

"I'm up for it if you are." He stuck out a hand. "Kyler Hale." He grinned, because the guy seemed a touch constipated, but he also kept glancing at his son like he'd never seen the kid before.

Paige had that effect on people.

"Austin Williams. Pleased." The man had a firm, solid, no-bullshit handshake. He approved.

"Good to meet you. So, where do y'all like to eat? Paige and I are just settling here, and we don't know the area yet."

"There's a great diner—burgers, sandwiches, milkshakes, soup."

"Chicken nuggets?" Paige asked.

That child was made of chicken nuggets.

"Oh, yes. And they have crispy French fries."

"Oh, yum." She beamed at Mr. Williams. "I love those."

"Me too!" Little Dallas bounced, so much happier.

"Come on, you bunch of hooligans," Kyler said. "Food." A milkshake would make his day better.

"Yes, and your spare pair of glasses are in the car, okay, son?"

Dallas nodded and glanced up at his dad. "I'm sorry, Pop. Honest."

"You didn't do anything wrong," Williams said firmly. He liked that. "And you have a very good new friend who had your back. How cool is that?"

"Really cool, Pop." Dallas gave Paige an adoring stare.

Oh man. He bit back another grin. "I'm in the silver Dodge. We can follow you?"

"Sure. I'm in the gold Acadia."

"Nice."

He got Paige loaded, and she started up as soon as he got in the truck.

"Daddy! Did you hear that lady? She called me a liar! That Wayne boy is so mean! He was going to poop on Dallas!"

"You did good, baby girl. I'm proud of you for standing up for Dallas." He would talk to her later about the rules here. Once she'd calmed down.

"He was all alone and everyone said mean things about him. Uncle Wacky says that those are the people you have to love the hardest."

"Uncle Wacky is right." Wacey Beame was his best friend, albeit old enough to be his uncle, not Paige's. Still, he gave good advice. "You did a good job, sweetheart. You ought to be proud."

"Yes, sir. I like him. He's real smart. He reads all the time. He gave me a book of my own."

"What did he give you?" He realized he'd been so busy with shit the last few weeks, he hadn't sat down at dinner and talked with Paige like he usually did. He had no idea what was going on with her.

"It's called the *Dinosaurs Before Dark*. It's a whole bunch of books called *Magic Treehouse*, and he said they are second-grade books and he told me the words I didn't know and said I was smart!" She bounced in her car seat. "Did you hear? He thinks I'm smart!"

"You are, baby girl." But that meant next to nothing in the rodeo. Book smart. His girl was a hand, and she knew horses and goats and cows and trailer hitches. Books were a new frontier. "I'm proud."

"Thank you! Do you think Dallas likes chicken nuggets?"

"I've never met a kid who didn't. And if not, I bet he likes spaghetti and garlic bread." A diner favorite of his girl's.

"Cool. Or mac and cheese. He eats peanut butter jelly for lunch, just like me!"

"Does he? That's good." No peanut allergy then. That boded well.

"Uh-huh. He has purple jelly, not red, but that's it."

"Grape, I bet."

"I like strawberries."

"I hear you." He followed Williams to the diner, then coasted to a stop.

"It smells good. Can I have Coke?"

"Nope."

"Durn."

"Milk, lemonade, or orange juice, okay?"

"Okay, Daddy." She took his hand after she hopped out of the car. "And you hafta have water with whatever you get too."

"That's the bargain." He loved a Coke or a cup of coffee, but she'd decided he needed to not be dehydrated.

"I love you. You got to meet Dallas! Finally!"

Had he really not been paying attention?

"I'm so glad. We need to start sitting at supper again so you can tell me things."

"I would love that, Daddy!" She beamed at him, bouncing on her way to the door.

God, he needed to slow down and remember what was good and right in his life. She was his light.

"Come on, Paige! We can sit in my favorite booth!"

Williams smiled at him as they met at the entrance. "I had no idea he had a favorite booth."

"Right? She told me she's been waiting for me to meet Dallas for-ev-ar."

"They've known each other for twenty days of school, you know. Two. Zero." The guy rolled his eyes.

"That's an eon at their age." Time had no meaning in kindergarten.

"Maybe more. He wanted to give her a copy of his favorite book. I hope you didn't mind."

"Not one bit. She was so excited. She's not used to folks calling her smart." He twisted his lips wryly. "Not that she isn't wicked smart. She's just been a rodeo kid, and this is her first experience at formal schooling."

"Sure. Sure. My boy grew up surrounded by books and not a lot else."

They joined the kids at the big, round booth, and he grinned. This would have been his favorite too.

"Hey, Dallas! Austin. How are you guys?" The server came over, handing out menus. "Welcome, all. Is this your first time, honey?" she asked Paige.

"Yes, ma'am. Do you have chicken fingers?"

"Do we? They're only the crispiest."

"Oh, yay! What's your favorite Dal?"

"I love the mac and cheese best. Do you like mac and cheese?"

"I do!" They high-fived, and he shared another grin with Dallas's dad.

"I recommend the fried chicken sandwich and the patty melt."

"Damn. I like both." He eyed Austin Williams. "We could pull a kindergartner and split two things."

"Works for me. You into fries, slaw?" Okay, that was easy peasy. He liked that about the man.

"I love a fry, but a side of slaw is not amiss. We'll just graze." Okay, maybe he was making him a new friend too. Or at least a dad he could deal with. That would be great.

Paige had rodeo friends for the summer. Cousins in Texas. But a school friend was like gold.

The kids were talking a million miles a minute, and Kyler stared a second, trying to figure out how his tomboy baby girl had ended up being friends with this skinny, kind of nebbishy little boy.

Dallas and his father looked just alike—tall and beanpoleskinny, with great big dark eyes with black eyelashes that folks would pay to have. They both had a mass of wild, ebony curls a bit too long for hat-wearing.

They both had glasses, and where the guy had grown into his features and was now bordering on being pretty, the little boy was all elbows and eyes. Just elbows and eyes all swollen from that bruise.

Jesus Christ, kids were assholes, and he knew it, but nobody should get beat up that bad at school.

"So what do you do for a living?" he asked because that was what a polite guy did. He made small talk, knowing some of it didn't apply to him. Hell here, most of it didn't apply to him.

He couldn't figure out why the guy's cheeks went vivid red, and why all of a sudden he couldn't look at him. "I'm a writer."

"Oh that's cool." And intimidating. Shit. "You write books?"

"Yes, I do. I write books. I'm a…novelist."

"That's cool." Kyler swallowed hard. He was not going to bring up the fact that he was a guy who periodically let a photographer take pictures of his belly real close for romance novels because, well, no one needed that kind of reputation, and this guy was a novelist.

That was different than romance books, right?

"What about you?" Austin asked, and Kyler shrugged.

"I'm a cowboy. I have a little ranch, but my money-maker is in leather work."

The guy's blush went damn near purple, and he didn't get it. "Leather?"

"Yeah. You know—saddles, chaps, custom work."

"Oh?" Those dark eyes focused on him. "Okay, that's cool. So, you literally make saddles? Like from scratch?"

"I do." And somehow he felt...cool. Like he was someone fascinating, and it straightened his spine.

Right now he was awful busy building his house and getting his workshop in order, trying to decide if he was going to run a couple head of cattle or focus on horses and llamas.

Kyler still wasn't a hundred percent sure how he ended up lucky enough to have land in Aspen.

Thank God that his Uncle Billy'd had two surviving family members—him and Paige.

The parcel of land wasn't huge—thirteen and a half acres, but it was fenced, it had improvements, they were lucky enough to be on municipal water, and the pastures were green.

It was too good to walk away from. So he was building a house and a workshop. He was gonna raise his baby girl here.

It was going to be amazing.

"I don't know where I thought saddles came from, but I guess I assumed a factory."

"Some are. But I do custom work." And when he got back to work, he would make damn good money on commissions. He did bull ropes and chaps and saddlebags and all sorts of shit...

And he wondered what kind of leather Austin Williams had thought he meant.

"Daddy, can I have a pancake on the side?"

He raised an eyebrow. "You can either have the pancake or you can split a piece of pie with me at the end."

Paige tilted her head, the expression in her blue eyes one of pure calculation. "What kind of pie?"

The server brought their drinks, smiling. "We have apple, cherry, and chocolate cream today."

"Chocolate?" Now her eyes widened. "Okay, I'll have pie."

"Good choice." He winked at her, making her laugh.

"I think we'll share a chocolate-covered Rice Krispy treat after, hmm?" Austin offered, and Dallas perked up.

"Okay, Poppy!"

Paige tilted her head. "Why do you call him Poppy?"

"That's his name."

"Oh." Paige nodded. "My daddy's name is Kyler Justin Hale, but I get to call him Daddy. He calls me Punkin."

"What do I call him?" Dallas whispered.

"You can call him Mr. Hale, buddy. Is that okay?"

Kyler nodded. "Or Mr. Kyler is fine, too. Whatever works best for you, Dallas."

Paige locked eyes with Austin. "What should I call you, sir?"

"Mr. Austin?" Austin seemed a touch surprised by being asked. Maybe Dallas just didn't have other kid friends or family around.

Paige beamed at Austin. "Thank you. Do they have coloring pages here, Mr. Austin?"

"I think so. We'll ask when she comes back, hmm?"

"If not, we can turn these placemat papers over and make our own," Dallas whispered, like he was afraid that Paige would mock him, but she lit up.

"You are the coolest buddy *ever*!"

"We have crayons in the car if we need them," Austin told him.

"Oh, good. I don't have the bag of tricks with me today." When he and Paige had been on the road all the time, he'd carried a bag with some puzzles, colors, a couple of books, and one of those tic-tac-toe games with the pegs and holes for ease of playing.

But he'd cleaned out the damn truck. He'd have to put it back in.

The kids were talking again, and the drinks and coloring pages and crayons came, and both Dallas and Paige seemed to be in heaven.

"I really appreciate that she's being good to Dallas,"

Austin murmured under his breath. "School's been hard, on the social scale."

"I bet." He scooted a little closer to Austin. "It has for her too. She's used to adults, and to being the center of attention, I figure. The other kids don't get her as much."

"Well, I know someone who told me on the second day of school that she was his new best friend forever." Austin whispered low. "I thought she was a figment of his imagination."

"Oh, man." He glanced at the kids. Yeah, he could see where Paige, with her larger-than-life western wear, her double braids, and her big blue eyes, could sound like something out of a book, not a real girl.

The server brought more coloring sheets, and eventually their food, which was solid and comforting and tasty. He'd come back here.

"This is a good choice," he said. "Thank you."

"This is our go-to. I'm not much of a cook, but I try. Unfortunately, what I do like to cook, the kid won't eat, so we come here more than I would like."

Interesting. "What do you like to cook?"

"Asian food. Lebanese food. Indian food. Thai food, which I know counts as Asian. I tend toward the sour spicy end of the food spectrum, I guess." Austin shrugged as the words tumbled out of him. "He falls into the macaroni and cheese, grilled cheese, chicken nuggets, spaghetti, normal kid food end of the food spectrum."

"Paige could eat chicken nuggets breakfast, lunch and dinner, but she's not picky."

"I like oats for breakfast, Daddy, oats and pancakes, bacon, sausage, waffles..." Paige grinned at him. "My mama makes the best waffles. Did you know that Dal here don't got no mama."

"No?"

"Nope. He was hatched from an egg."

He glanced at Paige, then at Dallas, then at Austin, who

was sitting there with a smooth-as-glass expression on his face. "An egg?" he finally got out.

Paige beamed, so pleased to tell him something he didn't know. "Uh-huh. They put a seed in an egg and then? He was hatched. He don't got no mama. Only. Mr. Austin."

"I had a surrogate," Austin explained with a chuckle. "So yes, there was a sperm and an egg and an embryo and then? A surrogate."

"Oh."

Austin tapped the rainbow ring on his index finger. "Yeah. Oh. Hopefully that's not an issue."

He blinked. "No, sir. Not one bit." Shit, he'd never met anyone who'd had a baby by themselves. Even he and Henley had tried to make a go of it, and they'd both known that was doomed from the get-go. "That's pretty brave, having a kid alone."

Austin chuckled. "Well, it didn't seem brave at the time. On occasion since then, it has."

He rolled his eyes, because he was a single dad too. "Yessir. That I do understand."

Austin grinned at him. "There had been a long-term relationship. It simply didn't last past the few packs of small diapers."

"Paige's mom and me... We knew it wasn't that kind of a thing. But we caught pregnant, so we tried hard. And then we figured out how to be apart and give Paige what she needed. She's a good... egg," he teased.

"That's amazing. Is she local?"

"No. No, she travels. She has a condo in Dallas. We worked it out so Little Bit will spend some time with her in the summer, and then for now Henley will come here on the big holidays and visit."

"Momma and I talk every day," Paige said proudly. "You can borrow her if you need to, Dal."

"I don't guess I need a mom, but thank you. Is she nice like you?"

"She's a racer. She's tough and pretty. She bought me a horse."

"Wow."

"You can come see her. Her name is Penny."

"Like *Penny's w Day*! Except he's a puppy..."

"I like puppies too. Daddy says when our house is built, we can have one."

He glanced at Austin, who was grinning. "Yeah. We're building a house on some land I inherited. It's taking a while, let me tell you."

"Oh, I can only imagine. We have a cat and a condo close to town."

"Nice." What else could he say to that? Then it was time for pie, and they got two slices to split with the kids. It was weirdly... domestic.

Still—a cat? Really?

Men had cats?

"Can Paige come over for trampoline, pizza, and movie time tomorrow?" Dallas asked his dad. "Please. My room's clean."

"I—Let me talk to her dad. Maybe she has plans."

"Daddy, can I? I love pizza and movies."

"Let us adults talk a minute, baby girl." He would be fine with it, if Williams was, but he wasn't about to just say yes. This was important, teaching her that parents had the last say. "Are you even having pizza and movies tomorrow, Mr. Austin?"

"Tomorrow is Saturday. Saturday is trampolines at ten thirty, and then pizza and movies at the condo at noon. Paige is more than welcome, as are you, of course."

"That would be great if it's not an imposition." He could

check out the guy's condo, make sure it was safe for any future visits.

"Sure. This is a first time. I think that would be...best. In case she needs you." That made absolute sense.

"I agree. So if it works for you, we'd love to come. What can we bring? Or should we cover the pizza this time?" Fair was fair. If you did something at someone else's house, you brought something.

"How about you bring what you'd both like to drink, and we'll work it out? Did you want to meet at the trampoline park? I can text you the address."

"That sounds good." Neutral ground to start. He approved. This guy thought about things.

"Perfect." He wrote a phone number on the back of a business card and handed it to Kyler.

"Thanks." Kyler put it in his shirt pocket, then handed over his debit card when the server came over to ask if they needed anything else.

Williams did the same, and soon they were all standing in the parking lot.

"Okay, baby girl. Say goodbye to Dallas. We'll see him tomorrow."

"Bye, Dal! I'm going to read another chapter tonight!"

"Okay. I'll wear my red dinosaur shirt tomorrow!" Dallas waved and took his father's hand.

"I'll text you the addresses, and you'll have my details. Thanks!" Austin waved and took Dallas over to the SUV, the little boy trying to skip and coming off awkward as hell, at least until he did a handstand and hopped to the car.

This was not your average child.

At all.

"I appreciate it." He took his baby girl's hand, glad the catastrophe had brought about something good.

Paige held on to him, jabbering away ninety to nothing, and he did love to hear that excitement.

He needed to remember to listen to it and get out of his own head.

"Oh, Daddy. Daddy, do you like him? Isn't he nice? He shared his macamaronis and—he invited me to his Saturday!"

"I know! I think he's very nice, and I can see why you defended him." And the dad was damn intriguing too, somehow.

"He's sad, a little, but he is nice, and Uncle Wacky is going to be proud that I listened. And Daddy!" She stared into him. "It worked! I was nice, and he is my friend now."

"It did." He grinned. She had a lot of her momma in her. She was a little... hard to get to know, maybe. Goal-oriented. Focused. So for her to listen to Wacey about how to make friends and apply it meant she was growing up.

Lord have mercy, he wasn't sure he was ready for *that* jelly.

D*ear God,* Austin prayed. *Please let me get through today without totally geeking out about the fact that my son's only friend in the world's dad is the hot-as-fuck cover model for my hot-as-fuck books about a hot-as-fuck cowboy. If you could do this for me I would really appreciate it. And I would promise not to write any more kinky books, but it would totally be a lie because I have to pay my rent. Love Austin.*

Dallas was so excited he'd already had an asthma attack this morning, causing his breakfast to come back up in a rush, and Austin was so tempted to cancel the whole thing.

When he even suggested it, the tears had started, of course, and they hadn't been crocodile tears. No, they were real tears with snot.

So Austin figured this really meant something to his little boy.

"Do you think she'll come, Poppy? Do you think she'll really come?" Dallas gave him a worried glance.

"Well, son, she said she was going to be there. So did her daddy, so I would assume so." How the hell did he know?

He did know that if they didn't show up, Austin was

going to get a tire iron out and say that he needed another cover shoot and then go beat the son of a bitch to death.

Before...after...something with pictures.

There had to be something with pictures first. The pictures had to come first.

God, he had a headache. He stopped and poured himself a big cup of coffee.

"It's going to be fine, Dallas, don't stress this. Why don't you go put on your shirt?"

"I wanted to wear the red one."

"Well, you threw up on the red one. Don't you have another red shirt? I'm sure you have one more red shirt somewhere. In your dresser. Do you want help finding it?"

Dallas shook his head, frowned at him. "No, I can do it."

"Well then do it. We have to leave in like five minutes."

"We can still have pizza this afternoon, right? You won't tell about the throwing up part."

"No, you threw up because you were wheezing. It's okay. You're not sick. It's just your asthma. Everything is fine. Go find your red shirt. Now. Please. Before I have a stroke."

"Okay, I will. Thanks, Poppy. I love you."

"I love you too, son." Weird and wonderful and goofy and brilliant and not the most athletic and a little lost in a huge world—Austin adored his boy.

God, his life had changed in going on six years. He'd been with Christopher, then, and they'd decided to have a baby. Months of planning and hoping and expecting had built up, but it hadn't taken long—a week?

Not even, maybe a few days, he couldn't really remember now—before Christopher had seen this tiny, red-faced, struggling-to-breathe baby who already needed asthma treatments, and had said, "Man, I didn't sign up for this. I knew about the sleepless nights, but this? I'm not, I'm not into this."

Austin had thought, into what? Being a father, being a

caregiver, being a human being? What exactly aren't you into, you lousy piece of garbage?

At the time, he hadn't even said it.

He'd been too tired, too scared, too overwhelmed. Not to mention too fucking pissed off. So he simply said, "Get your shit and leave."

In fact, that was the only thing he had ever said to Christopher again.

Every single response he'd given to anything Christopher had said to him from that point on had been *get your shit and leave*.

And he'd meant it.

And he'd left, and that had been that. Now they were in a condo in Aspen rent-controlled by dint of the owner being a fellow author friend. And Dallas had a bestie.

Who had better show up at the trampoline park.

By the time Dallas found the shirt and got his shoes on, they were almost going to be late, so he texted the cowboy, just to make sure it was all going down.

<*On our way. We're running a few minutes late.*>

He got back, <*Ditto. Paige wanted to wear her little dress and suede jacket, and I had to explain at length about trampolines and pants.*>

Austin snorted. Okay, he liked this guy's way with words.

"In your car seat, buddy." He strapped Dallas in and off they went.

It was an easy drive, and Dallas was in an amazing mood now. Ramped up from his inhaler and ready to go.

"You excited, bud?"

"Yes, sir, I am. I'm ready too. Did you know that Paige is a cowboy?"

He'd only heard it like forty-seven thousand times. "Really? Does she have a horse of her own?"

"She does, and so does her mama. Her mama has lots of

horses. They are very fast. Her daddy rides horses that aren't ride-y horses."

"Yeah? Do you remember when I took you to the rodeo that one time?" So Mr. Hale was a bronc rider?

"Uh, it was dirty."

"It was. Do you remember the poop on the bulls?"

He could see his little persnickety boy's nose wrinkle. "Oh yeah, I don't like it, Poppy, I don't like poop."

"I don't think anybody does, honey. It's sort of like a thing."

"Did you ever want to be a cowboy, Poppy?"

He shook his head. "No, baby, all I've ever wanted to do is be a writer."

"And that's what you do. I think I want to make robots."

He could see Dallas waving his arms in the rearview. "I think robots are cool. I think that would be fine."

"Robot guys and cowboys, can they be friends?" Dallas asked.

"Anybody can be friends with anybody." He really didn't have a whole lot of friends who weren't writers, but he did have friends, theoretically, who weren't. That photographer friend. And a cover artist friend. Okay, so all of his friends were writers. Fine. But he wasn't going to tell that to his son.

Dear, Dallas. I'm a giant dork and I live in a fantasy world like ninety-nine percent of the time, so I need friends who do the same otherwise I feel weird. Also, they understand my need for coffee and pajama pants. And late-night therapy sessions involving imposter syndrome. Somehow I doubt that Joe Blow Cowboy would be into that.

But he could be wrong. What did he know?

They parked, and he could immediately see the big duallie and the man with the cowboy hat. "Looks like they're here, son."

"Oh, yay!" Dallas started to struggle free of his harness.

"Wait for me, bud."

"Hurry up, Pop!"

He chuckled, this enthusiasm so new. Usually if they went out, Dallas brought a book. Hell, so did he. They read together at the diner. Or they would go to the library.

This was better though. Dallas needed a friend. It didn't escape him that his son had chosen the roughest, toughest cowgirl in the West.

But he supposed they called them clichés for a reason.

They met Kyler and Paige in the little entryway, and Austin had to force himself not to ogle again. It wasn't even that the man was so hot, although he was oh-my-God-so-hot.

It was that Austin had seen way more of Kyler than was reasonable.

Not only that, but he knew how hot everything was in a three hundred pixels sort of way.

The simple fact was, in his head, that body belonged to Maverick Johnson, the hero of his series.

Not Kyler Hale, single dad.

The juxtaposition was too damn weird.

He was going to have to get over it, but that wasn't going to happen today. Possibly not even tomorrow. "Hey, guys."

Dallas ran to Paige. "Hey! You came! Are you ready to jump? We're gonna jump. I love to jump."

Austin gave Kyler a nod and kept his eyes above the jawline. "I promise I didn't give him coffee."

"You sure about that?"

"Pretty sure. This child and caffeine are not compatible under any circumstance. I also did not give him anything with maple syrup this morning for breakfast, because I am a kind and thoughtful human being who did not want to unleash his sugar monster onto the world."

Kyler kind of gave him a raised eyebrow. "Paige had Lucky Charms."

Dallas stared at Paige. "No fair. You get Lucky Charms? Pop says no sugar cereal for me."

"Only on special occasions. You know how sugar makes you. Besides, let's go jump." He didn't want to have a discussion about weird food issues in front of the Marlboro Man.

It wasn't that he was all oh, let's be persnickety, it was more that he had a lot of work to do. And he really, really couldn't handle Hyper Dallas.

Austin figured if he couldn't handle that, then who could? Why should the teachers and the public have to deal with Hyper Dallas?

Dallas 2.0?

The Dallasator.

Dallaszilla.

Hmm. He liked it.

Dallas, the Eater of Worlds.

"Pop, where'd you go?"

He chuckled. "Sorry, Dallas."

"Come on!" The kids ran to the front desk, and he and Kyler followed.

"How's it going?" Kyler asked. It was very polite and oh so stilted. He got it. They had barely met, and while their kids were buds, they were adult strangers.

"Good. He's been very excited."

"Oh my God, so has Paige. She changed clothes a dozen times. We finally settled on her little stretch jeans so she didn't show her damn underwear to the whole world."

He broke out laughing. "I never thought of that sort of technical difficulty of having a little girl."

Kyler handed over a debit card at the desk. "Yeah. It's a thing. And like, riding a horse in a skirt? Chafing. Especially bareback."

"Oh, dude..." That would *suck*.

"Yeah." He got a wry grin. "But she wants to look good on

occasion. I explained that her momma wears leggings under a skirt..."

"She's close with her mom, you said."

Kyler nodded. "Yeah. It's nice. It's good for all of us, you know. We're not like...it wasn't an ugly separation. Everything was on the up-and-up. We're all happy."

Lucky fucker. "That's exceptional. Seriously. No bullsh— Baloney." Austin rolled his eyes at himself. "Seriously though. I think that's cool. I wish I could have had something like that, but that wasn't in the cards."

The kids took off their shoes, handed them over and took off like bats out of Hell, climbing up and jumping and jumping and jumping.

It was early enough that the bigger kids weren't there, so there weren't a lot of bullies. And they could play around and wear their butts out.

"So you do this every Saturday?" Kyler asked.

Austin found himself staring into the bluest eyes he thought he'd ever seen.

Honestly, they weren't like this generic kind of smoky, someone-drew-a-blue-chalk-on-a-piece-of-concrete-and-smudged-it-out-and-that-was-the-color-that-was-left-behind-blue.

No. Kyler's eyes were intense—almost as bright as something out of a video game or a science fiction movie. But not scary, not fake. They were real.

And it was unnerving and wonderful and he was going to write this. God, why had he made Maverick's eyes brown and not blue?

It wasn't fair. Shit, the man had asked him something.

"Yeah, every Saturday. It's something physical that doesn't stress him out. He likes it. The people are very nice. I can get some admin work done if I want to, or chat with people, people-watch." It wasn't spending time with Dallas, exactly, but he still felt like it was worth it. "As you can tell, my son is not particularly athletic."

"Oh, he's fine. I know lots of guys who look like him that are plumb famous. I wouldn't worry about it if I were you." Kyler chuckled. "I wanted to say thank you for inviting us today. It means a lot to Paige and me. She was a little bit worried about going to regular school, and apparently—from what I understand—she and *her* Dal have become the best of friends." Kyler rolled those gorgeous eyes.

Be good! Pay attention.

"I have to admit, I've been so busy building house that she sits and talks at the dinner table, and I sit there sort of like a lump. Half the time these days, our dinner is whatever I can pick up at the drive-through."

Okay. House.

There was an actual subject that they could discuss without him thinking weird thoughts. Yeah.

"Tell me about your house."

"Well, I was damn lucky to inherit a little plot of land from my uncle. He always said he would leave it to me, and damn if he didn't." Kyler shook his head. "I'm also lucky that it's in a horsey area, so no one has developed up around us."

He nodded, thinking of some of the Roaring Fork areas he knew like that.

"So anyway, I got about thirteen and a half with improvements, so I'm building out a house with a few extra bedrooms and a nice big kitchen and a wraparound porch, and then we'll have a barn and a workshop for me." Kyler's cheeks went dark pink under his tan. "I ramble on about it."

"Dude! Ramble. I have a rent-controlled condo. It's literally the definition of nothing special." No self-deprecation, now. He worked for himself.

"Hey, in this valley, that says something." Kyler grinned. "I don't suppose they have coffee for very sadly in-need dads?"

"They have a fancy coffee shop, even. You want my discount card? You get punches for each coffee." He loved their hazelnut lattes. That was his Saturday breakfast.

"Sure. What would you like? I'll grab it for you." Kyler seemed so easy in his skin.

"Just tell him it's for Austin. They know." His cheeks were burning as he dug the card out of his wallet and handed it over. "I'm sort of a regular. I'll get the next one, promise."

"No worries." Kyler laughed as he walked away, and that gave him the view of the butt. Fans had written odes to this man's ass. Literally poems about Kyler's butt, even though they thought it was Maverick's butt, or they thought of it as Maverick's butt, and it wasn't Maverick's butt; it was Kyler's ass, but it was still pretty fucking intense there in the jeans. Kind of amazing.

This wasn't fair. He hadn't been laid in six years. Six years *almost*. And yet here he was. With Maverick who was Kyler. At a trampoline park with their children. God was evil. And had a sick sense of humor. And personally, Austin did not approve.

Okay, that was a lie.

He approved a lot. There were five covers to the series of books Kyler was on. Butt. Hand holding the buckle. Amazing jawline and collarbone. Holding the hat with face shadowed. And then one that was a nice slice of the entire backside, top to bottom. Complete with broad shoulders and one firm, tight, little butt cheek.

Five covers, with five different fantasies. It had never occurred to him that he was going to have to interact with this person like a human being and not a fantasy photo.

"Pop, Pop, look at me! I'm jumping. I'm jumping."

He nodded, glanced over, tearing his eyes away from said denim-covered heinie. "You are doing a good job, bud. Way to go, Paige."

That girl could jump. And she was damn fearless too, throwing herself up and down and all around like she had no concern about broken bones or sprained joints or messed up hair or broken glasses.

"Thank you!"

It was unnatural and kind of cool.

Kyler came back a few minutes later with coffees and some kind of bag of pastries. "Here you go. And I hope you're okay with either an apple fritter or a chocolate croissant."

"I can happily nom either one."

"I've never met someone who says 'nom' out loud," Kyler teased, those eyelines crinkling right up.

"Stick with me for more amazing word plays."

"I'll do that." Kyler sat and opened the bag out like a plate, letting him choose which pastry he wanted, which was pretty chivalrous. Or whatever. And he needed to stop thinking that way, because Kyler's ex was a woman.

Rule number one: do not lust after the straight dude.

Especially not the straight dude who had the cowboy thing going on who could absolutely, one hundred percent kick his butt. Because honestly? Butt-kicking? Really not in his list of skills.

Now if someone needed poison pen letters, he was a boss. You need someone to cut you short in a very carefully worded letter to the editor? He was the man.

"You wanna split them half and half?" Kyler asked him.

"Sure why not? I like them both."

Kyler stared over at the kids while Austin was trying to mangle the pastries with the plastic knife that had all the sharpness of the wit of a blustering politician. "She seems like she's having fun."

"She does. I think they both are. There is some energy being expended up there. If only we could bottle it..." And there he proved he was a dyed-in-the-wool, dork single dad.

Because that was something middle-aged people said to one another when talking about young people. God.

He was going to have to start writing space operas where it didn't matter that all of his references were meant for another generation.

Space operas or cozy mysteries.

Possibly greeting cards. He could totally rock a greeting card.

"I hear that. I think that about every little beast, animal or man, that I come across. If only they knew how much they were going to want that energy in a few years' time, and yet here they are out there spending it like there were no lean times ahead." Kyler's tone was so wry.

"Well, I know it's silly, but maybe we can hope for no lean times ahead." Pollyanna much?

"Sure. Sure, why the hell not? I could go for no lean times." Kyler grinned and winked at him. "I made some money on the rodeo circuit, but there have been...I mean, there were some real lean times back when I was starting out."

He knew better than to ask if there was actual money to be made in the rodeo, because after all, that was what he did. He wrote about rodeo cowboys. To be fair, they were mostly naked, and usually what they were riding were not bulls or horses, but still, Austin had done his due diligence.

"So, did you ever get to go to the NFR?" See him show his knowledge.

"I did. I mean, I was low man on the totem pole, sitting right on the bubble, but I did. Now, Cheyenne? Denver? The big stock shows. Santa Fe... I did well at those events on a day-at-a-time basis."

"Those are some big purses, right?"

"Yeah." Kyler chuckled. "Enough to build a house. I still have to take odd jobs to cover the rent in town though." Those cheeks went dark again.

"Hey, that's a lot of cash. I get it. It's a lot."

Also, I'm the odd job. Me. Odd job.

"It is. But I'm happy with the progress. We'll be in before the holidays and the weather gets bad."

"That sounds lovely." Trite, but he didn't wince. He smiled and stuffed a bit of croissant into his mouth so he would shut up.

"It will be nice to get back to making saddles. That's where I really want to put my time."

"You'd said. That is cool as all get-out. That's something that's crazy unique."

"Yeah. I mean, it's a niche market for sure." Kyler winced. "Careful, Paige! Don't forget that some kids are smaller than you."

Like mine, he thought, though Dallas was laughing like a loon.

"Sorry, Daddy!" She helped Dallas back up to standing. "Jump! Jump!"

Dallas bounced, grinning and waving his arms.

"Lord, they're going to be sweaty."

"Yes. But after pizza and a good old-fashioned Disney film? They'll be exhausted." And that was the goal.

"Sounds good. Just not *Encanto*, please. I have nightmares about that Bruno song."

"Oh, lord. You know how many times he's sung that? Right now he's into *Cars* and *Brave*. He wants siblings." Like he could afford that.

"So does Paige. She keeps saying how cool it would be to have a little sister to dress up." Kyler rolled his eyes. "Like a doll. I swear, I was not prepared to raise a girl."

"No? I lucked out—Dallas and I are two peas in a pod. So, barring his asthma and my weak ankles? We match up."

"Oh, she's a cowgirl, my daughter. But she's pink and

sparkly and just... She's wild and wonderful and I wouldn't give for her."

He tilted his head. "Give what?"

Kyler blinked. "Anything. I mean, it's an expression."

"Oh." That was a new one on him, and it was so going in a book. "Cool. I love that."

Dallas came to him, sweat beaded on his face. "Pops, I need a drink, pretty please?"

"You bet, buddy." He pulled a bottle of water out of his bag. That kept Dallas from trying to get a Coke or something.

"Thanks. Is there one for Paige?"

"Of course. I brought four." He lifted the second bottle out and held it up.

"I'll try to remember to bring stuff next time. I wasn't sure if outside things would be allowed. Thank you." Kyler took the water, then waved Paige over. "Come get a drink, kiddo."

"You can bring in things, otherwise it would cost a fortune. No glass bottles. No food or drink on the play floor."

"Got it."

"I'll be sure to fill you in on the rules from now on. I hate to be unprepared, so I don't want you to have to be."

"I appreciate it, man. I have a feeling we'll have our share of play dates." Kyler nodded to Paige, who was showing Dallas how to gargle words with the water. Then burp.

Dallas was giggling like a mad thing, staring at Paige with pure adoration.

Lord, that was adorable, and he hoped it didn't crash and burn too fast. Paige was bright and athletic and chatty. She was bound to make girl friends pretty quick.

Still, Dallas needed practice at making friends, one way or the other. He wasn't going to stress it too terrible hard.

"Okay, I wanna jump a little more." Paige gave Dallas a hopeful glance. "We can go slower."

"I can do that." Dallas beamed, then took her hand, and off they went.

"She's a sweetheart." Such a good little heart, to be so kind. "Thanks for bringing her out."

"Hey, I just wanted to know where the good pizza was." Kyler winked.

"Ah. We're going to order and have it delivered. It'll be easy for them to chill and relax." He wished Dallas had a place outside to play, but he didn't.

"Oh cool." Kyler tilted his head. "They're starting to droop."

"Yeah, well, they've only expended like five billion calories." He winked over it. Kyler. "There's a method to my madness." He raised his voice. "Yo, Dallas, you ready to have some pizza and watch movies?"

Dallas was red-cheeked and sweaty, and it was good because he was kind of worried there would have been an asthma attack or something after this morning's scene. But no, he was doing great.

"I'm ready, Pop. Can we have pepperponies? Paige likes pepperponies on her pizza."

"Sure." He glanced over at Kyler. "Now that's love, man, because. Dallas hates pepperoni."

"Oh, maybe we should get a half cheese and a half pepperoni."

"I think that that is the absolute wisest decision. You'll have to think about what you take on your pizza. I figured I'd get one for each of us." He personally was a chicken, pesto, and jalapeno pizza kind of guy. He would bet all of his pennies that was a little too queer for the cowboy. So he'd let the poor guy pick his own pizza.

His character Maverick took all the meats, no veg. Which was really very, very bad for your intestinal system, but not something one mentioned in romance novels so...

The kids both drank some more water, and then they headed out, children yammering together, two peas in a pod.

"Come on, let me give you the address to the house, in case we get separated."

He texted their address.

"Can I ride with Paige, Pop?"

"Well, buddy, your car seat's in the car. We'll go separately, and then she'll be there in just a second. It'll be okay." God help him.

"Yeah, I think that would be best, kiddo." Kyler chuckled. "I like the barbecue chicken pizza if your place has one, or I'll take the supreme."

"You got it." He was surprised at the easy veggie-accepting. He stuffed a very pouty Dallas into the car seat, waving as he headed out.

Kyler followed him easily, but didn't ride his ass, which he approved of. In fact, he would feel comfortable with Dallas riding with the guy.

All in all, if Kyler wasn't his cover model, well, he would be super pleased about this whole situation.

Chapter Six

Kyler hummed along with the radio, tapping his fingers on the steering wheel. He was headed to the Cowboy Wanted office to pick up a check. They would have paid him electronically, but the photographer had sent a check made out to him and one made out to them for their commission. So he would just go grab it.

That way he could make the next payment to his contractor. Man, he was ready to get out of that apartment and into his house.

He pulled in and parked, walking inside to see Tom sitting with his feet up on his desk, earbuds in, playing the air drums.

God love a small business.

He tapped on the desk, and Tom almost fell over in his chair. He righted himself, then laughed, taking out his earbuds. "Sorry. Sorry, I was jamming. Koby is off grabbing lunch. The kiddo in school?"

"Yeah. So I'm running errands." He rolled his eyes. "Being a single dad is nuts."

"I bet it is." Tom dug in his desk drawer. "Here's your check."

"Thanks, man."

"So are you open to more work like that?"

He pondered that. "I'm not sure I would want to do more book covers. Like, the photographer was pretty good about explaining to me how it would be nice for this series to have an exclusive model."

"Hmm." Tom blinked at him. "I guess I can see that."

"Now, if another job comes up you think I'm good for? I'm in. And if you know anyone who needs custom chaps or saddles..."

"Oh, I can always farm you out for that. I'll put the word out. That way maybe you can have some Christmas jobs."

"That would be amazing." Kyler grinned. "I'm grateful, though. This gig got me over the hump on my house."

"How's that going?" Tom asked.

"You know how it is. Slow and steady for weeks, then crazy for a week while a flurry of shit gets done." And those flurries were so damn stressful, going over plan changes, approving budgets, and cutting checks.

"Well, you got this, man." Tom gave him a boxer stance, then a one-two punch in the air.

"I do. Paige is so damn excited. She keeps telling me what she's going to do with her room and all..." And some of it was kind of scary. Rodeo princess meets Wednesday Addams, of all things.

"She's a hoot."

He'd had to bring Paige to one of his meetings with Tom, and the two of them had been fast friends. She thought he was like Dallas.

"So smart, Daddy," she'd said. "Just like Dal."

Somehow that little boy had become the benchmark for all manner of things.

"Okay, I need to head out. Thanks for this," he told Tom.

"No problem, Kyler. And like I said, I'll get the word out. Do you have a card for the leather work?"

"I do." He pulled out his wallet and handed over a business card. "Thanks."

"Always happy to help." Tom winked, then put his feet back up on his desk.

He headed out to his truck, then coasted into town to deposit the check. There were at least three to four more errands he needed to run, but damn, he was starving. Maybe he should stop and get a burger. Or a slice of pizza. Something junk food as hell.

His phone buzzed, and he checked it as he slid to a stop at an intersection.

It was a picture of Henley on her racing mare, turning the third barrel before they would race home.

Then he got another buzz. *<Won the short go this weekend. 15.9>*

He checked his rearview, but no one was waiting, so he tapped out a response. *<Way to go, lady. Big arena?>* 15.9 seconds was a little slow, but some arenas, like Houston or Cheyenne, had a long final run for a barrel racer.

<huge. best time after me was 16.8>

Damn. Almost a whole second lag. She was a superstar. So he sent her a shooting star emoji.

<I'll call P tonight>

<Cool. Talk then>

He got moving again, because someone was behind him, and politely tapping the horn rather than laying on it.

He pulled off when he saw a parking place, then googled where he could get a good, greasy meal. So many of the restaurants in Aspen were gourmet-type things, and they were pricey too.

"New York Pizza," Kyler murmured. "By the slice to go? Hell yes." He'd had pizza with the kids and Austin, sure, but he could eat it every day. He headed back out and in twenty minutes, he was munching his way through two huge slices of pizza with pepperoni and mushrooms.

Damn, that was a fine thing. He tried hard to give Paige good, nutritious food, but sometimes he remembered he'd lived on fair food and fast casual hamburgers and fries for years when he'd been on the road.

He licked his fingers, feeling much more up to the day. This was his life now. He was a stay-at-home, work-from-home dad, and he ran errands while his kid was in school.

That seemed nuts, but then… Well, Austin was the same way, right? He worked from home, he was single dad. He got it, and it was kinda nice to have someone who was in the same boat to talk to. To compare experiences.

And God knew, Dallas was a hoot.

The thought had him pulling out his phone and texting Austin. *<want to do dinner tomorrow night? I could go for a burger>* He knew it was a school night, but Paige didn't have anything going on.

He wasn't sure Austin would answer. Hell, he wasn't sure he should be texting about anything but kid plans…

<Love to. What time?> came back almost right away.

Kyler grinned wide, his fingers flying as he set up their meeting.

It was good to have someone like Austin for sure. Unlikely as it was, he thought they were going to end up good friends.

***

"Guys, y'all are not going to believe this."

Dallas was in bed and Austin had a glass of wine and was in the space he used for an office, Zooming with his online sprint group that met once a week.

It had been a walk-in closet/pantry thing, but they'd taken

down a lot of the shelves, and squeezed in a real wood desk and a fold-out chair.

It wasn't fancy, but it was his.

"What?" Lilian was in Detroit, and she was way into dark romance. She was married to a pastry chef and sent the most amazing cookies every now and again.

"Are we all here?" He didn't want to have to explain about Kyler more than once.

"All five of us," Dom growled, even as Helena waved the hand that wasn't holding her new baby. "Spill."

He sipped his wine, then grinned. "You know how I showed y'all my new covers? *The Maverick* ones?"

"Yeah, those are blistering." Erin wore her glasses, and he could hear the quiet tap-tap-tap from her keyboard. Someone was on deadline. "What about them?"

"I met the model."

Everyone stopped, then Dom leaned forward. "No shit?"

"No shit." He explained about Paige and Dallas, about the trampoline park. Everything.

"Dude!" Helena grinned at him. "Is he...you know..."

"Queer? I don't know. I called a gay cowboy want ad place, and he did the job, but I'm not getting super gay vibes."

"How's your gaydar, though?" Lil wasn't helping.

"Not bad. I mean, we have only dealt with each other about our kids, you know? We've only talked about Paige and Dallas. He's literally a cowboy."

Horses and a ranch and a pickup truck and poop on his boots.

"Is he as hot in person as he is on the covers?" Dom asked, and Austin shook his head.

"He's very real in person. Very not polished and flexed." There was no doubt Kyler was the model, but the real man was...less than perfect.

It was incredibly hot, in a weird sort of way, and Austin was not sure how to process it.

Erin blinked up at her webcam. "Have you told him?"

"God no."

That caused an uproar, everyone spurting out their opinions, which everyone had.

"You have to tell him!"

"I can see the posters from here!"

"When he finds out, you're going to be sorry."

"He'll be embarrassed. Just drop it."

Finally he held one hand up, interrupting them. "I don't know what to do, y'all. I'm serious. I mean, the big thing here is that this is the first kid that my boy has even so much as spoken to. His first friend." He met all their eyes, one window at a time. It occurred to him that he wasn't sure what he looked like, whether he was making eye contact with any of them, or none of them, if he wasn't staring into the camera. God. "I'm serious, guys. I'll do damn near anything to keep this little girl talking to Dallas."

Erin shook her head. "It's been that bad, huh?"

"Three pairs of glasses since school started. It's *September*." He shook his head, his eyes filling with burning tears. "It's like he's got a target painted on him psychically or something, and he's not— I mean, he's not an asshole. He's just a smart little boy."

"Oh, honey." Lilian sighed. "Smart is a target all itself and, you add to that, he's small. He's a reader, a little fantastical."

Dom nodded, his voice like gravel. "You need to teach that kid how to run or to fight back. Can you put him in judo?"

"He's already in trampoline and gymnastics. Do you know how much that costs? I'm not—I can't put him in something that he doesn't like. I'd have to take him out of one of the other classes." Dallas loved trampolining and he loved gymnastics. Austin couldn't deny his boy those. "This is not a karate kind of kid. He's just not aggressive."

Erin chuckled. "Sounds like that little girl is, though."

He nodded. "So, apparently, she grew up a rodeo kid—like honest to God, traveling all the time, no home to speak of rodeo kid. Her mother races horses, and her dad is a bronc rider."

And Austin was beginning to understand there was a lot of stuff he didn't know about being a cowboy, or rodeos, or a lot of things he thought he probably ought to understand. At least it was good research, really.

If a little gross.

And smelly.

"So wait—" Lil frowned at him. "You say he's not gay, but you hired him through a gay company that farmed him out to a gay photographer..."

Austin shrugged. "Honestly, honey, I hired a service because I knew them. We'd met at a gay Chamber of Commerce meeting here in town."

Dom snorted. "Fucking gay chamber."

"Hush you. I have no idea if the photographer was gay. It didn't come up. I never met her. Everything went through Tom at the service."

"Oh. Well, that makes sense?" Lil didn't sound convinced.

"Where's her mom?" Helena asked.

"They're split up, and he has custody. The mom apparently felt like Kyler's more of a homebody, and that's really all I know. I mean, we're not all that close yet, to share such deep information. I do know that the mom is in the picture, but not in the immediate picture."

"Wow. That's kinda harsh. I mean for a little girl to be without her mom all the time." Helena cradled her baby, a tear sliding down her cheek.

Austin didn't know. Paige seemed pretty good to him,

when it came right down to it. "Her daddy adores her. Seriously. He's raising an amazing human."

"That's what's important, then." Erin sighed. "You do need to tell him. He's going to figure it out, eventually."

"I know." He did, but he was liking having a local friend, even if Kyler wasn't all that close yet. "I guess we ought to get to sprinting, huh?"

"Ew."

"I've already got a thousand words," Erin muttered. "Let's do this, you hooligans."

Right.

Sprinting.

Fuck all this real-life stuff. It was time to play...

"Okay, tell me when you're ready, y'all, and we'll start the timer..."

Chapter Seven

"Honey, stop bouncing. They'll be here." Kyler grinned at Paige, who was wearing a pink T-shirt that read, *Be nice to me. My Momma is crazy and not afraid to use i'*, a pair of sparkly butt jeans, and her pink boots.

Dallas and his dad were coming out to meet Paige's horse before they headed out to the Ute Trailhead to do a bit of hiking. So he had her sneakers in the truck.

Pizza had been a real success, with the kids munching pizza and watching *Moana* while he and Austin chatted. It had been... nice to talk to another adult. It had made him feel real, which these days, with every damn thing in flux, was a good thing.

"I know, Daddy. I just want to dance."

Yeah, she'd tried to wear a pink tutu over her jeans...

"Well, come here." He opened the music app on his phone, and "Take it to the Limit" by the Eagles started playing. "Waltz with me, kiddo."

"I love to sing with you, Daddy." She came right to him,

her baby feet on top of his. And he danced her around, his heart full.

This whole thing was hard. Building a house. Trying to make things work, starting a ranch, getting his business back off the ground. But it was worth it. He was doing it for her.

"Do you think that Dallas will like Penny? Or do you think he's going to be scared?"

He imagined, with all of his heart, that Dallas was going to be terrified. But he had to give it to that little boy. He was going to brazen this whole thing out. And if Paige liked horses, he was gonna like horses, damn it.

"I think he's going to be fine, baby girl. He's very excited."

"Me too. I can't wait for them to meet. And then he could have a horse. He could name his horse Maui. Or Eragon. Or Pebbles. And then we can ride together all the time." Her blue eyes glittered.

Somehow he doubted Austin was going to be willing to get a horse. But, hey, you never knew. The guy was kind of cool and weirdly fascinating. The condo Austin kept would be...sparse even. Modern and super clean. Except for the fact that obviously the man believed that books were furniture, because they were stacked everywhere. Bookshelves, sofa tables. Coffee tables. Everywhere. It blew his mind.

And it didn't seem to matter what kind of books. There were westerns, sci-fi, and fantasy. There were nonfiction books. There were the top ten from the *New York Times*. Manga. Comic books. Kids' books, chapter books. It was like a library.

And what was weirder was that Austin knew where everything was. Kyler admitted he'd seen a title that he kind of recognized and had asked for it to see if Austin had any idea, and man, not even a hesitation. He'd walked over to a stack, run his finger down it, and gone bloop, and then offered to let Kyler borrow it.

That was the strangest damn thing he'd ever seen. But also it kind of suited Austin, who was kind of like something out of some kind of mystical movie Doug Jones played the main character in. But more sensual than creepy.

He liked the look of Austin.

A lot.

That probably wasn't something to be thinking about right now, but it was true. And every so often he caught Austin watching him a certain way. The way that maybe indicated interest. Like, in a sexy way.

It boosted his ego a bit. Maybe a lot.

He danced his girl in another circle and ignored the SUV pulling up until Dallas came running over.

"What are we doing?" Dallas half-shouted.

"Dancing, kiddo. I taught Paige to waltz a bit ago."

"Poppy dances!" The little boy exclaimed, his eyes huge. "He did ball dancing." Dallas glanced at Paige and wrinkled his nose. "The shoes are so funny, and he wore sparkly shirts."

Paige tilted her head. "My momma wears sparkly shirts to work. Did your dad do that for work?"

Austin nodded. "Uh-huh. When he was a teenager. Then he got very tall. Ball dancers aren't very tall. And they have to dance with girls. And my Poppy doesn't dance with girls. My Poppy dances with boys."

Paige frowned. Looked confused for a moment. And then before she started asking questions she pointed to the fence. "You wanna go see my horse? Her name's Penny. She's very pretty."

Oh thank God. That was the last thing he wanted to get into right now.

He wasn't a homophobe at all. In fact, he was sort of more than a little interested in exploring that side of him, but that wasn't the point. He wasn't ready to explain this whole thing to his daughter. Whose mother was a barrel racer.

He had a life. He couldn't deal with that right now. He had enough. Thing was, he couldn't even like, tell Austin that he didn't want... What? For Austin to be who he was? That was stupid.

But Dallas wasn't even being political or shocking. To him, this was just life. And there was nothing wrong with that. But in the circles that Paige lived in, sometimes it was considered bad.

God, he had a headache.

"Hey, man, I brought, um, snacks and backpacks. And water." He got a smile. "And sunscreen. And hats. Dallas is so excited and a little terrified. But he's going to do this and..." Austin tilted his head. "Are you okay?"

No, no, he was in the middle of this great big philosophical quandary all of the sudden. He was not okay. "I'm fine. I just have a headache."

"Oh well, I've got Tylenol, Advil, and Motrin in the car. Along with baby aspirin. In the first aid kit in case someone has a heart attack."

"I don't think I'm heart-attacky now." Maybe he'd stroke out, but not a heart attack.

"No, I meant like, we're walking down the street and someone has a heart attack and the car is close. You know, it's just that's part of the thing. You're supposed to have them in a nicely done first aid kit."

"Well, you are a good Boy Scout, aren't you?"

It must have come out meaner than he had anticipated, because Austin's cheeks turned a dark, embarrassed red. Angry, almost. And he shrugged. "I guess I went by what the recommendations were. That's all. So this is your land. It's charming."

Well shit, now he'd hurt the guy's feelings, and he really hadn't meant to. Christ, Austin hadn't done anything wrong.

And Kyler hated the fact that he was uncomfortable when the man hadn't done a thing to him.

"It is. Like I said, I've inherited it, but I'm really trying to make it something. I appreciate you coming out. Paige is so excited for Dallas to meet Penny. Is he excited too?" *Will you forgive me for being an ass? Because I didn't want to, and I did and, fuck...*

"Excited. A little nervous. Okay, a lot nervous. But trying very hard to be brave. I told him that. He wasn't expected to do anything but watch if he didn't want to. He doesn't have to interact with the horse if he's freaked out. I hope that's all right with you. But I'm not, you know, I'm not going to have him panicking and getting himself or Paige or the horse hurt because he's scared."

"That's totally fair." They walked toward the barn. It was makeshift, but it worked for now. "Paige is good about that. She helped with a petting zoo on tour this past year."

That got him a wide-eyed stare. "As in worked it?"

"Sure. I mean, she wasn't child slave labor or anything, but I pick my battles. I wasn't about to tell her she couldn't visit the goats and chickens and Daisy the donkey every day."

"Daisy the donkey, huh?" Austin asked and glanced at him, grinned. "That's cool. What other kind of animals do you think you want to raise here?"

"Oh, the girl wants big birds and cows. She saw a miniature once and wanted that too."

"They make miniature cows? For teeny tiny steaks?"

"I think as pets." Hell if he knew the whys. He just knew Paige wanted one of everything. "Wait for me, kiddo!"

Paige had taken Dallas into the lean-to, which was fine, but he wanted to be there for the meeting.

"Okay, Daddy!" Her tone was more wicked than obedient, but he'd take it.

They followed more slowly. "So is there anything you

want to know about the hike today?" He was reaching, but he didn't want an awkward silence.

"I googled it. It seems like something doable for the kids and me. I brought snacks and water."

"Cool. I did too this time." Hiking he knew, and he and Paige had picked out this activity, so it seemed only fair.

"Dallas loves walking and hunting for rocks and different things."

"Oh, good." Whew. "And you said he's not allergic to peanut butter."

"Nope." Austin chuckled. "We sound stilted. Are you wigged-out that I'm gay?"

"No." He made that very firm and not loud and shocked. "I'm really not. I was just surprised at Dallas. In my circles, no one comes out with it, so it kinda made me go, huh. And then I was rude."

"Dallas has no idea that he should be worried, so..." Austin shrugged his shoulders. "He's innocent, I guess..."

"He is, and that's great." He tried a smile. "We good?"

"Yes. Totally. You don't have to worry. We're allowed to have friends." That wink was naughty.

"Oh, hey." He felt his cheeks heat. "So are cowboys." God, Henley would give him no end of shit about this.

"I'm glad. It's fascinating getting to know you."

"Thanks. I feel the same way. You're not like anyone I know."

"No? I can say the same."

"All my friends are cowboys," Kyler said, and he tried not to sound all wry. "I was on tour so much..."

"All my friends are writers. I know tons of them from all over."

"Wow. I mean, I guess you meet all sorts on the internet? We cowboys meet at rodeos, but I'm the same way. They're from all over." They did have things in common, oddly enough.

"Yeah. I have friends all over the world, even a few in Denver, but…it's challenging, you—"

"Daddy, come on!"

"Coming!"

Austin gave him a smile. "Whoops."

"They get impatient. She wants to show off so badly."

"I understand. She needs Dallas to like her life too."

He sure hoped the little boy would.

"She does." He led the way into the barn. "Okay, Paige. Let me get her halter on."

"Okay, Daddy." Paige ushered Dallas away from the stall. "This is Penny. She's my good horse. My momma bought her for me."

"She's real big."

"She's nice. I promise. Don't be scared."

"Well, honey, he shouldn't be scared, but he should be cautious. What do I always say?"

"They're big enough to hurt and smart enough to be trouble."

"Exactly. Show him how to feed her a carrot."

"So, you gots to make your hand real flat, okay. And put the carrot in the middle, like this." Paige showed how to give Penny her treat, no stress.

"Oh. Okay." Dallas sounded worried, but he did it, and he giggled when Penny's soft lips brushed over his hand. "Oh, you're pretty."

"She likes when you say that." Paige stroked her forelock, the star on her forehead.

"She knows a good many words," Kyler told Austin. "She loves the word carrot, huh, Paige?"

At the word, Penny whinnied and tossed her head, nodding yes.

Dallas's eyes were the size of saucers.

Paige grinned and held out her own piece of carrot. Penny crunched it right up, way less gentle with her girl, who knew all her limits. "Good lady. Such a pretty baby."

"She's very brave," Austin whispered.

"She doesn't know any better," he murmured back. "She knows as many animals as she does people."

Hell, maybe more.

She was the progeny of two horsemen. It was in her genes.

"So, this is Dallas's first chance. Especially not with anything that's not a cat or a dog. My mom has a poodle, but she doesn't—she's old. The poodle. Not my mom."

Austin made him chuckle. "Where does she live?"

"She and my dad live in northern New Mexico, right over the border. They bought a big piece of land up there, and they live with one of my sisters."

Kyler hadn't imagined that Austin had family, somehow. "Do you have a big family?"

"Two sisters and a brother, so big enough, you know. There are four of us." Austin's mouth twisted. "My sisters and brothers are all very...charismatic. So are Mom and Dad. Football. Softball. Soccer. Acting. They're very outgoing and traditionally attractive. I'm the outlier, of course. My brother Houston has two little girls and a wife—Kayelle. Antonia, who Mom and Dad live with, is married and she has one baby and is working on a second with her husband. Then Wimberley is a stuntwoman in LA."

"Really? No shit?"

"Really. She's a hoot. Absolutely fearless."

Kyler couldn't hardly imagine it, really. This quiet guy had a stuntwoman sister. Go fucking figure.

"That's pretty damn cool. I mean, shit, I think you being an author is really neat. Seriously. How many people actually make a living at that?" He was fascinated by the idea.

Especially recently.

"Not a ton. I'm very lucky that I have loyal readers." Austin shrugged and offered him an oddly nervous smile. "Seriously, it's a great job."

"That's— Whoops." Kyler stepped forward and moved the mare sideways. He would bet neither kid even noticed, but that kept them from getting squashed as Penny swung her big butt around.

Austin stared, and Kyler was proud of him for not reaching out and snatching Dallas up and running. Kyler could see by the way Austin's fingers curled in that it was a huge temptation.

Paige laughed when she bumped Penny with her shoulder. "Sometimes she's clumsy like me." So Paige had noticed and was correcting Penny. Good girl. He breathed a sigh of relief.

"You're not. You're just...so fast." Dallas beamed at Paige. "Sometimes your feet outrun your brain."

"All the time!" She giggled harder. "And you're always careful where you put yours."

"Uh-huh. Always. Sometimes it's no fun."

"I think you're fun, Dal! I think you're great."

Dallas flushed and grinned. "Thanks."

Kyler rolled his eyes. Lord save him from new besties. "Come on, Paige. Let's get Penny out in the paddock for the day, and then we can go hike."

"Does she just go outside? What if it rains? What if she gets scared?"

"She has access to the inside. See that opening over there in that roof that leans? It's called a lean-to," Paige explained. "She can get under there."

"Lean-to." Dallas giggled. "I like that. Poppy! It's a le-ee-ee-ean-to."

"It is! I like that word too."

"What's your favorite word, Mr. Kyler?" Dallas asked.

Did people have favorite words? This seemed like a game they played a lot, based on the way Austin and Dallas looked at him, and he didn't want Austin to think he was a moron, so he cast about. "Latigo."

"Oh, that's a good one! Poppy!" Dallas beamed. "What does that mean?"

"It's the long strap of a western saddle. It's a Spanish word."

Okay, that was hotter than advertised. He grinned. "Bingo. What's yours, Dallas?" He hoped to hell he knew what it was when Dallas said it.

"Labyrinth!" the little boy cheered. "I love that word!"

"Oh that's a good one. Good movie too." He winked at Austin, because he heard that soft chuckle.

"Oh, yes. One of our favorite oldies but goodies."

Kyler wasn't sure Paige was quite ready for *Labyrinth*...

"I like Appaloosa," Paige said. "Such a neat sound."

"Appaloosa? That's a..." Dallas scrunched his face up. "A... a...a horse! A horse with a spotty butt!"

"Yes!" Paige grabbed him and squeezed him. "How did you know?"

Dallas and Austin spoke together. "*Appaloosa Zebra*."

Kyler chuckled along. "Nice one. And what about you, Mr. Austin?" He took off Penny's halter to let her loose in the small pasture. He wouldn't leave it on and have her get hung up on something trying to scratch it off.

"Almost. I love the word almost." No hesitation at all.

"Yeah?" He tilted his head. "Why?" That one didn't make sense.

"Because it's the best plot device ever. Something almost happens or almost doesn't happen. It's a magical word."

"Okay, I can see that." And now he did. "That works. Y'all ready to hike? Sunscreen? Water?"

"Poppy made up a whole backpack!" Dallas was so proud of his dad that it was adorable.

"Did he?"

"Uh-huh. Snacks and water and bug stuff and all."

Paige grinned. "He's prepared!"

"Uh-huh. He always is. He reads all the books and on the computer about things."

Kyler had to wonder if Austin ever did "everything", or if he only read about it.

Which led him to wonder what Austin read about late at night, and that was probably a bad thing to think about. He made sure the gate was closed behind Penny, then grabbed Paige's hand.

"You going to follow us to the trailhead?"

"Sure, or we can go together. I'm easy."

"Well, let's move the other car seat to the truck, then." He was good with driving. That way if the kids got filthy it was his truck that got slimed.

"Sounds great to me. That cool with you, Dallas?"

"Super cool, Poppy." Dallas grinned at Paige. "I get to ride with you!"

"You do!" The kids sang the whole way, and Kyler was thankful he had the Disney singalong playlist on his phone so he could plug it in.

Austin knew all the songs too, singing along in a lovely tenor that made him grin.

That was adorable and made him like the man more.

They all piled out at the trailhead, and he gauged the kids' energy. "I think we plan on about a quarter to half a mile out."

"Sounds good to me. The kids can play and have a snack whenever we stop to turn." Austin chuckled softly, murmured. "I never thought I'd be on a playdate with Dallas."

"Right?" They had that in common. "Paige would rough-house with the other rodeo kids, but they saw each other just enough to breed contempt, not friendship, I think." Paige had been called bossy more than once...

Dallas, though, he was easygoing and sure seemed ready to have someone who was a friend.

"Well, I think she's wonderful," Austin said. "And so does Dal."

"Come get a drink, y'all," he said. "And get your sunblock on."

"We got spray-on, and it doesn't smell bad. Yay!" Dallas did a butt-wiggle dance that amused the hell out of him, and when Paige copied him, Kyler cracked up.

Soon enough, they were walking and the kids were running, skipping, singing, and examining every rock.

"Lord, thank you so much for inviting us. I can't tell you how much it means." Austin smiled at him, ambling along like this was the best day ever.

It kind of was, actually. The sun was shining, but there was a nice cool breeze, and spending time with Austin and the kids made him smile.

Austin fascinated him in ways Kyler had a hard time explaining, even to himself.

He breathed in deep, then let it out, tracking Paige as she almost wandered off the trail.

"Stay with us, kiddo. No going off on your own, okay? And the trail is what?"

"There for a reason. It protects the land around us," she chanted.

"That's it." She was learning her land conservation lessons well. It was kind of a passion of his.

"She sounds like you do this a lot," Austin said.

"She's hiked all over the southwest. From Texas and New Mexico to Nevada and Northern California. And now we're learning about Colorado, right, kiddo?" he called.

"Right!" She beamed at him. "I am a mountain girl. I'm

going to learn how to snowboard this winter. Do you like skiing, Dal?"

Dallas shook his head. "I don't know how."

"Oh. Well we should try it together."

Austin gave his kid a doubtful glance, but Kyler knew it was the little ones who blew out the world at the rodeo...

"Do you ski, Austin?"

"I have, yes. I haven't in six years or so. I've been crazy busy."

"Cool. I did Steamboat once during ski week. BP." At Austin's raised eyebrow, Kyler chuckled. "Before Paige."

"Oh, I like it. Maybe we can all learn together, huh?" Austin smiled at Dallas, who shrugged.

"I'm not good at it."

"How do you know?" Paige asked.

"I don't know!"

"Well, see?" Paige chuckled. "If you don't know, you don't know."

"But you don't know I can. What if I hate it?"

"Then you don't do it no more."

"Any," Austin corrected, then winced and shot him an embarrassed side-eye.

Kyler nodded. "Anymore, kiddo."

"Okay! Dallas, look at the little bird."

"Oh...so pretty..."

"Sorry, man. It's a knee-jerk reaction. I'll try to not."

"No worries. You beat me to it, is all." Lord, his ex would beat his ass if he let Paige get away with bad grammar. She was all about presenting herself well.

Austin offered him a grateful smile, which was much better than his unhappy face. In fact, Kyler wanted to see more of that smile. "I love how she is with him."

"She's just her, I reckon." He laughed. "But thank you. I

always hope I'm doing all right, and when she's making other folks smile, I know she's doing okay."

"She's incredibly brave and charming."

And he thought little Dallas was smart—serious and smart.

Dallas took a tumble then, tripping over his own feet, and everything froze for a moment while Kyler and Paige waited to see how Dallas and Austin handled those kinds of things.

"You okay, buddy?" Austin asked when Dallas sat on his butt, blinking.

"Um." Dallas glanced at Paige, who was smiling in an encouraging way. "Uh-huh. I'm not bleeding."

"Good deal."

"Here." Paige stuck out a hand. "I do that *all* the time."

Dallas took her hand. "Thanks. I saw a pine cone. A big one."

"Ooh. Cool. Where? We can put peanut butter on it."

"Peanut butter?" Dallas dangled for a moment when Paige yanked him up, but then they were off.

And Kyler was relieved that Austin had done a nice bit of let's-see parenting. "He's pretty brave for a kid who says he can't ski."

"He's scared of anything new, but really, if he tries, he's pretty athletic. He's got asthma, but the doctors are pretty sure he'll outgrow it."

"I can see that. I know a lot of guys who ride the rodeo who had it when they were young." He offered that, not sure what Austin would make of it.

"Yeah. I have a friend that's a competitive diver who did too. It's more a matter of stress." Just like it was nothing—no big deal.

Kyler nodded, because he had no idea what to say to that. Paige tended to sock people in the nose when stressed, just like her momma.

"Stress is wild on the body. So I try to keep him easy, but... maybe I do too much."

"Hey, I don't judge. People say I let her run wild." He had to shake his head now instead of nodding. "Maybe we'll learn from each other."

"Daddy! I need water."

"Sure, baby girl."

He had four bottles of water, and God knew what all Austin had in his pack... Hell, that was half the reason he'd decided to go easy on the trail. That pack had to weigh a ton.

"Oh, me too, Poppy? I'm thirsty."

"Sure. I have waters, snacks, whatever you need."

"Can we sit a minute?" Dallas waved at a convenient bench.

"Is that okay with y'all?" Austin asked.

"Sure." Paige would dance or run or whatever. And maybe have a snack.

They sat, and Austin pulled out hand wipes, a picnic blanket, and a Tupperware box filled with cheese and crackers.

Wow.

That was... wow. It should have seemed so fussy, but it was sweet, somehow. Like Austin would have gone to the trouble anyway, but that he was doing it for him and Paige added something to it.

"Oh, Daddy..." Paige blinked.

"I brought enough for everyone. There are strawberries and grapes too..."

"That's amazing, huh, baby girl? What do we say?"

"Thank you! Daddy brought peanut butter cheese crackers and Oatmeal Cream Pies."

His cheeks heated. "They hold up well if it's hot."

"Dallas and I love Oatmeal Cream Pies! We buy them for a treat."

Even if it was a lie, it was sweet to hear.

"We do too. Hiking is a special thing." He added his stash to the pot.

They had a little feast, Dallas perking up after food and taking Paige to play in the alpine meadow they were sat in.

"Thanks for this," Kyler said. "It was really nice."

"Thanks for the invite, man. I appreciate it. He's so happy."

"Well, we'll have to do something again soon, huh?" And hope that Paige and Dallas didn't break up before they got the chance.

"Sure. Absolutely. Dallas is talking about going to the movies for his birthday in a few weeks, and we always have pizza and trampolining."

"We do." He packed the trash away. They would take it home. Trail trash cans invited bad animal habits.

"Good deal."

"You have to show. Daddy! Look! Dallas can do a cartwheel!"

And he'd be damned if that little boy didn't just do one, no stress.

Kyler clapped. "That was very cool, kiddo! I like it."

Dallas bowed. "I'm here all day."

That made him snort. That kid was wicked smart.

Paige frowned. "Okay. So show me. I want to do it."

"Sure." Dallas grinned. "You start by putting your hands on the ground like this." Dallas bent and put his hands flat on the ground. "And you start with a little jump." He hopped his feet up and around. "That way you don't fall down while you learn."

He bit back the urge to call to her to be careful. He wanted her to stay fearless as long as she could.

"It's so hard. I leave him at gymnastics class."

"He takes gymnastics?"

"Since he was two."

"Wow. That's great." Paige would love that, he would bet, but he was also thinking about swimming for her. There was a great community center where she could go.

"The gym is really reasonable and low-key. I'll text you the info, if she wants."

"Thanks. I'd like that. We'll see which way she leans, right? She wants to do all the things, but I work to get her to pace herself." He winced when Paige landed on her ass, but she bounced right up.

"Sure. No pressure."

"Good job!" Dallas cheered. "I'm so proud."

She beamed, and they all chuckled. "Such an appreciation society."

"They need it, I guess. Kids are fascinating."

"They are, and it's nice to see her with someone who likes her so much."

"Daddy! Daddy, I did it!"

He applauded. "Way to go, baby! You guys about ready to head back?"

"No, but I know it's better to go back happy than poopy!"

Dallas cracked up. "Nope. No poop!"

Paige cackled like a giant bird.

Kyler shook his head as they headed back toward the trailhead. Lord have mercy.

He'd always imagined that having a girl wouldn't be as gross as having a boy.

Dallas and Austin were proving him wrong.

Chapter Eight

"Poppy!" Dallas came running out of the school, tears on his cheeks. "I want to go home. Now. Right now."

"Okay, okay, buddy. What's wrong?" Dallas hadn't been this upset in eons.

"Paige yelled at me, and said I was a sissy. Am I a sissy because I'm scared to try skiing?"

He bit back all sorts of things that tried to come out of his mouth. Most of them were anti-Paige, so he kept them to himself, because that was knee-jerk. He took a deep breath. Took Dallas's hand because his shoe was untied.

Then he spoke. "Of course not, buddy. And it's not nice to call someone a sissy. Or try to bully them into doing something."

"She says we're not friends no more. I want to go home. I don't want to go to trampoline tomorrow. I want to stay home."

"Hey, let's get home and have a little sit and maybe a cookie, and we'll talk about it, huh?" His job was to find out what had actually happened while having his kid's back. But he wouldn't let Dal make snap decisions.

After he got Dal in his seat, he texted Kyler. <*Kids had a fight. Fair warning*>

<*Crap. I'll come get her. She's supposed to be helping in the library, but I know she'll be a mess. Dal ok?*>

<*Crying hard. Says he dsnt want to go trampoline 2morrow. Call later?*>

<*Sounds good*>

He and Kyler talked quite a bit once the kids were asleep, so they could work out what was going on later. He felt like he had a little parental support there.

Austin sat for a while and gave Dallas time to calm down. Then he made a peanut butter and jelly sandwich. Strawberry jelly, crust cut off. Sliced into four triangles.

He poured a glass of milk and then headed in to see Dallas and have a talk.

Dallas was sitting in the middle of his bed, his *Goosebumps* comforter wrapped tight around him. Glaring.

"I brought us a snack to share. Can I sit?"

"You're the dad. You can do anything you want to."

"Dude, wouldn't that be cool? If I could do anything I wanted to? We could time travel together, you and me. I could snap my fingers, and we would be anywhere."

That almost got a smile, and Dallas, took a piece of the sandwich. "Anywhere. Like where?"

"I think we'd start in the Old West. We could be gunslingers together. And then when we were done doing that, we could go back to medieval times and see if there were dragons. I don't think I'd really be a knight, though. I think that that armor stuff had to get stinky and who wants to walk around clanking like an old rusty tin can."

He let himself wrinkle his nose. "Anyway, can you imagine the tetanus?"

Dallas's eyes went wide. "Tetanus. That's the lockjaw stuff. I wonder if knights got lockjaw."

Austin shrugged. "Right? Because there weren't any vaccinations. But, but we're going to visit, and we're looking for dragons."

Dallas nodded. "Okay. Also I want to go see a mermaid. What time were mermaids?"

He pondered that. "I'm pretty sure mermaids were medieval too, don't you think? Or maybe ancient Greek."

"Vikings. Were Vikings medieval?" Dallas asked.

"Well, Vikings are a people, so they kind of went like the whole time."

Dallas rolled his eyes. "No, that was cavemans. Neanderthals. Neanderthals were before Vikings."

"Fair enough, fair enough. Were Vikings before Egyptians?" He loved having these sort of talks with his son, not only because they were fascinating, but because if Dallas was talking to him, Dallas wasn't crying. He hated when his little boy cried.

"I think the Egyptians came first." Dallas frowned. "Can we look it up?"

"Sure we can. Can we talk a little bit about what happened at school first?"

His phone buzzed, but he didn't glance at it right now. This was about Dallas.

Dallas sighed. "I knew you would do that."

"Sorry, kiddo. You know how I feel about having all the information."

"I know." Dallas drew his knees up to his chest and wrapped his arms around them. "We were talking about what activities we wanted to do, and this winter they'll do a ski field trip as soon as there's snow."

"Wow. That's pretty cool."

Dallas's lower lip pooched out. "Snow is cold."

"It is that. But you liked sledding when we did it last year, right?"

"Yes. But that wasn't standing up on snow."

"Well, you don't have to learn all by yourself. I could help you. I mean if you're scared about falling down."

"I just don't wanna. I don't want everybody to be mad at me because I can't do it."

"But you *can* do things, dude." Austin hated this because he was afraid he was a part of this whole I-can't-do-things' movement on the Dallas front, and that wasn't right.

But then he didn't know what to do.

It was very frustrating.

He did want to yell because it wasn't Dal's fault, but he kind of wanted to yell because it was frustrating and… "You do gymnastics, don't you?"

"Yeah, but gymnastics are easy."

"Some people don't think so. I think gymnastics is hard. I can't even do a…" He waved his hand. "…walk over. And you can do flips and stuff on the trampoline."

"Nobody watches when I do that, though."

"I watch. Miss Michelle watches. All the different people at the gym watch." He gave Dallas a grin. "Why, you even have a little bit of a crowd that watches you on Saturday."

"Well…" Dallas chewed his lip.

"You don't have to, though. You don't want to ski, you don't have to ski. But it seems kind of silly to decide you don't want to if you don't know how to do it yet, because you might want to learn. Did that make sense?"

"No, Poppy, but it's you. Sometimes you don't make sense."

"Ask my editor; I don't make sense a lot." He winked at Dallas. "We could learn together."

"You already know how," Dallas shot back.

"I already knew how," he corrected. "It's been many years. Since before you were born. I'm pretty sure that my body has forgotten how. And I'm old."

Dallas pursed his lips. "What if I fall down?"

"You fall down all the time. I fall down too. It's part of skiing. Everybody is going to fall down. You have to be super fancy and to learn to do that swoosh thing that you see on the TV."

Dallas blinked at him. "Could you do the swoosh thing before you had a baby?"

"Yeah. But I really didn't have you have you, you know. Like I didn't lay an egg."

Dallas threw his hands up. "Ew! Daddy, that's gross. Don't talk about eggs. Dragons lay eggs. Chickens lay eggs. Platypi lay eggs."

"Platypuses," he corrected automatically. His brain, he was going, *is there something wrong with my child that he went to dragons before chickens*? He supposed it was better than going to snakes before chickens, but nobody ever said what came first, the dragon or the egg.

"Oh, Poppy." Dallas sighed. "I just want Paige to like me again."

"Hey, friends sometimes have words, kiddo. Tomorrow, though, I bet you're friends again."

His phone buzzed one more time, and he patted Dallas's knee. "Want to finish up your snack and then come down and play some Sorry?"

"Okay." Dallas grinned. "Go talk to Mr. Kyler."

He chuckled. "I'll see you downstairs."

Sometimes his kid was too smart for his own good. When he got downstairs, he heard his phone beep again. So he finally glanced at it and all it said was, *<chat?>*

So Austin went with it. He grabbed his earbuds off the table and popped one in. He called Kyler as he dug around in the hutch for the Sorry game. He really needed to reorganize. This was insane.

Kyler answered quick as a bunny. "Hey, man. This sucks."

"Yeah, no shit on that. Did you figure out what happened?" He guessed they needed to get it from both sides of the fight. Austin was worried that this is going to end up being more about Paige finding new friends now that she was settling. As much as he hated to admit it, Dallas was not the traditional cool child.

"They got into it over frigging skiing of all things. Paige is desperate for him to come to this skiing thing that she's talking about. She doesn't want him to go only because she likes the idea, but she wants to go really bad. So she got her feelings hurt when he said he wouldn't try. She just doesn't understand that not all people like the same things."

Austin started putting the game out as he nodded. "True that. I told Dallas that we could do some practicing together if he'd like. That way he can see how he does. He's terrified of yet another set of kids figuring out that he's not good at something and of them making fun of him."

"Yeah, that makes sense." Kyler sighed. "So I'm going to start taking her up to the pool for swimming lessons. I really think that she needs to know how, and I think she'd be good at it." Then Kyler chuckled. "Lord help me, she wants to do 4-H, she wants to go to gymnastics, she wants to do this skiing thing. It's just a lot, man."

Austin wasn't sure what to say, because Kyler sounded kinda grim. He didn't want to suggest that it was a money thing, but what if it was a money thing? It could be a money thing.

Seriously, Kyler was the one posing for photos for Austin's

covers. Maybe he should get more covers made. That would give him the incentive to write a new series about Maverick.

Although, could he write more books about Mav? He had no idea, but regardless he could get more covers. Maybe use them as posters or original art or something for his readers. It was a thing. And the books were selling well right now. "Well, there's no reason that she can't do all of them, I guess. Is there? Do you need her to have a ride?"

"Yeah, that's the biggest part. I mean, if she does trampolining on Saturdays, she does swimming on Wednesdays, and you said gymnastics is Mondays and Thursdays, 4-H is on Tuesdays I mean, and then there's Girl Scouts, there's skiing lessons there's—"

"Dude, dude. It's okay. They don't have to be busy every second of every day. That's what I tell myself. And let me tell you, I work at home too. So I get it. Everybody thinks that you have nothing but time and you can drag the kids around to everything. So do what you need to do, in my opinion, of course. And you know, I've been a dad so much longer than you have, ha ha ha."

Austin rolled his eyes at himself.

"Yeah." Kyler blew out a breath, but his tone was more upbeat when he went on. "Yeah. I think that makes a lot of sense."

"Cool. So sit down with her and make decisions. There can be one social club and two athletic things, or two social things and one athletic thing. That's what I did with Dallas. He has trampolining, he has gymnastics. That's three days. He's not interested in Boy Scouts."

"Does that mean you're not going to let him come to swimming with Paige?"

"I tell you what. I'll drive them to gymnastics. You drive them to swimming. We'll meet on Saturdays for trampolining. And then? You and Paige have to work out 4-H and or Girl

Scouts. What do you think? Dallas is not ready to commit to the ski camp, but I'll go ahead and get the deposit put down in case he decides he wants to do it. But don't tell Paige because he might change his mind. He's little. Boys are younger than little girls, you know that."

"God, don't I know that. I think that my little girl is more mature than I am." Kyler laughed at that one.

"Well, we won't get involved in their little spat. They'll figure it out. They're good kids. Are we still meeting at the trampoline park tomorrow morning though, do you think?"

"I think Paige would be in hysterics if we didn't. She's got her routine. Horseback riding. Trampoline. Pizza, movie, and crashing out at your house is really her jam on Saturday. That's when she misses her mom the most."

And bang. Right there, again, was this graphic illustration of how Kyler was not queer. And was not Maverick. And of how he could not look upon his son's best friend's father with lust. That was bad.

He got all wrapped up in what felt almost like co-parenting recently and let his fantasies run wild.

Cowboy wanted, and all that...

He took a deep breath. "Well, if we can keep to the routine, it will be good for her, and for Dallas. He really doesn't want to be at odds with her. So I'll massage him into coming tomorrow, and we'll maybe get a big cookie with our pizza."

"Damn, now that's near and dear to my heart. Cookies." Kyler's chuckle made the hair rise on the back of his neck. It was almost sexual. "Okay. That's the plan then. If anything changes, I'll text."

"And vice versa." He grinned a little. "See you tomorrow."

"Yep. Thanks, man. You talked me down out of the tree."

"I live to serve. Bye."

"Bye."

They hung up, and he checked to make sure Dallas wasn't lurking on the stairs listening. Which he wasn't. His kid was pretty polite about waiting for adult conversations to be over before coming into the room...

Not to mention it took him forever to eat a sandwich.

Chapter Nine

"Paige, honey, don't forget your hat!" Paige had chosen Annie Oakley as her costume this year, complete with one of her mom's old fringed suede jackets, which on her was a coat, and a pair of gauntlet gloves. She had the weird round cowboy hat too, that was in all of the old pictures of Annie. She had a miniature toy rifle for the pictures with Dallas, but she would have to leave that behind for the trunk or treat.

"Got it." She snagged the hat out of the truck, then skipped up the walk to Dallas and Austin's condo.

"Good job." He texted Austin rather than ringing the Ring, because Austin had said he would be upstairs making sure Dallas was in his Sherlock Holmes costume, which was pretty historically accurate, and therefore pretty damn complicated.

"Are you excited for the night, kiddo?"

"Uh-huh! I've never had a townie Halloween."

Oh, God help him if she said shit like that.

"It should be fun. Trunk or Treat, then supper, then trick or treating—"

"Then movies and candy and a sleepover!" Paige jumped up high enough to fly. "Yeehaw!"

"Lord have mercy, girl. Don't kill yourself acting like a kangaroo."

"I'm just excited, Daddy." Her blue eyes flashed when she gave him an over-the-shoulder-under-the-hat look. Patented by her mom.

"I am too!" He was tickled as shit that she and Dallas had weathered their first big two fights. The one over skiing, the other over matching costumes. Dal had no intention of going as Buffalo Bill, and Paige had no idea who Irene Adler was...

"Helloooo." Austin opened the door, his butler costume kind of hilarious. And oddly... cute. "May I announce you, madame?"

Paige glanced at him, gaze a touch panicked. "Daddy?"

"This is Miss Oakley, if you please." He was totally willing to make the save for her.

"Of course. Of course. Mr. Holmes, you have a Miss Oakley here."

"Elementary, dear Jeeves. Elementary." Dallas was absolutely adorable—deerstalker hat, long coat, magnifying glass, and a meershaum pipe that blew bubbles.

"May I take your hat and gun, Miss Annie?" Austin winked, inviting Paige to share the joke.

"What would Momma do?" he murmured.

Paige lit up like the cowgirl in *Toy Story*, then took off her hat with a flourish. "You got it, pard."

"Thank you, m'dear. Please come in and have a seat. Mr. Holmes will see you soon."

Dallas's giggles filled the air. "You look great, Paige!"

"Thanks!" She shook out her hair." Daddy even crimped me so I'm like the picture. Show him, Daddy!"

He pulled out his phone to show the reference picture of

Annie Oakley. She was a brunette where Paige was blonde, but he thought it worked.

"Wow! Great job!" Dallas gave her a worried glance. "Do you like mine?"

"You're, like, the best! You're the best detective ever."

Dallas simply beamed.

Kyler grinned, watching them compare treat bags. "So what's your Sherlock?" he asked Austin. "Basil Rathbone? Downey Jr.? Benedict Cumberbatch?"

"Oh-ho. You're a fan, I can tell." Austin grinned. "I approve. Who's yours?"

"Oh, I asked first."

"I have a shock blanket in the office."

Oh, very nice. "You do, do you?"

"Yep. I bought it at an online auction."

"I might have once announced that I'd had a fight with a chip and pin machine." And no one he'd been with had gotten the reference to the British TV version of *Sherlock*.

"Oh, very nice. I approve." Austin bowed again. "My favorite bit is the last episode of season one and the first episode of season two."

"Yeah?" He could see that. They were fun ones. "I love season one. And most of two..."

"Three had its moments," Austin murmured.

"We don't talk about four," they said in unison, then cracked up.

"Daddy! Are you almost ready?"

"Yep. Bathroom for all, though." He had no idea what the situation was at the trunk or treat, and Paige was weird about port-a-johns.

"Yes. We'll all go together? I have chili—spicy and not—and cornbread for supper before tricks and treats."

"Yummo!" Paige twirled again.

"Sounds great, Austin." Kyler gave him a warm grin. The

man was organized as hell, and he appreciated that. He was also cute as hell in that penguin suit. Like in a way that kind of made Kyler stare.

Why on earth was he fascinated by Austin's butt? It was ridiculous. He'd stared before. Who didn't, right? And he'd been surrounded by Wrangler butts, male and female... But Austin was so easy to be around, so warm and human and real. It was bizarre.

Maybe it was the goofy bowtie.

It just made things adorable.

Maybe he needed to let himself lean into that a little. Henley had always said he was sure as shit bi, the way he checked everyone out.

"Okay," he said after a bathroom break. "To the wagon!"

"Off we go to get our candy!" Paige cheered.

"Candy!"

"Mmmm. Candy."

His body tightened all of the sudden, because Austin's tone was damn sexual. Shit. "What's your favorite?"

"Peanut butter cups." Austin grinned back. "I have a bag in the kitchen up high."

"Mine are Almond Joy."

"That's positively medieval of you."

"I know. It was my Granny's favorite, and she passed it on," Kyler said with a shrug.

"I love that. Seriously. What about you, Paige?"

"Green apple Jolly Ranchers!"

"I like Snickers best," Dallas said very seriously. "Last year I got a whole one!"

"A whole one? Really?" Paige's eyes were huge. "Whoa."

"I know, right?"

They chattered about candy and costumes and what they might see tonight all the way, the kids buoyant right now. He kept stealing glances at Austin as the man steered them to the rec bus lot that would take them to the rec center. That was why he hadn't driven; there was no parking at the event and that would drive him nuts.

"Come on, you hooligans. Let's go see what there is to see!" Austin helped Dallas out, and the kids held hands until it was time to get on the bus.

They boarded with a witch, a rabbit, and a passel of zombies, which made Paige stare, and they debarked to a carnival-like atmosphere that made both kids squeal.

"Oh, Daddy! Look! It's a *party*!" Paige was going to pass out.

"I know. Wow. So where do we start? Dallas, you're the expert."

"At the beginning."

The library had a bookmobile, a sign-up sheet, and a free scary book and a bag. It was adorable, and of course it was a library that started it.

Of course.

They hit all the hot spots, the kids bouncing and almost running, making them work to keep up. But Austin never lost his smile, never got frustrated. He was a good guy.

"Poppy! That truck has Halloween push pop toys!"

Austin chuckled and grinned. "O. M. G.! Go for it!"

Paige glanced at him, gave him a confused little half grin. "Is that cool, Daddy?"

"Uh..." He had no idea. He grinned. "Let's go see."

"Right. Let's see. Dal likes some cool stuff."

"Paige, I mean, Annie! They have a cowboy! And a pumpkin!"

"Oh! Can I have the pumpkin?"

"Uh-huh."

"Hey, I get it now." Kyler had seen those toys with the bubbles that pushed in and out. He had no idea they had a name.

Paige and Dallas had to choose carefully, and Austin watched them with a fond expression.

"He's going to be my little collector. I can tell."

"Paige is very excited about having a room. She wants to be able to fill it with stuff. When you're on the road all the time, you have to be careful with that, you know?"

"I can't imagine. I am a bit of a homebody, and I do like my things…"

"I love that the house is in the dry." They were, in, too, even if it he was still saving money by installing a lot of the finish work by himself. "It's nice to wake up in the same place."

"Yes. And to be close to your horses, and not have any rent, right?"

"Yeah. Yeah, that's helped a ton."

"Good. Good. That's great to hear." Austin's cheeks went super pink, and he tilted his head. Could be the cold, he reckoned. But he seemed almost embarrassed every time they talked about anything that remotely smacked of money.

Kyler wondered if Austin thought he was destitute. Austin never fussed about letting him pay his half, not ever. But he did seem to get flustered when the situation arose.

By the time they were done, the kids were dragging some, and it was time to go refuel. Damn, he hoped Austin's chili tasted as good as it smelled in the slow cooker.

"Let's go eat, and then, if y'all want, we can trick or treat, okay?" Austin started moseying them toward the car.

"Okay!" Dallas's little voice was half volume to what it had been before.

He winked at Austin over the kids' heads.

"Are you guys excited about movie night and camping in the front room?" Austin asked, and Paige nodded.

"I am. I like chili too. Is it real hot?"

"There's two kinds. Hot and not," Dallas explained.

"Okay. I like not too spicy, but I can eat the not hot with some salsa..." So sweet his girl. He could eat shit that would peel paint.

"You can do it up however makes you happy, Paige. Cheese, onion, Fritos, cornbread, salsa, sour cream. You do you." Austin simply didn't sound worried.

"Cool! You're so nice, Mr. Austin. Momma says I can eat it the way she makes it or go to my bunk."

"Well, I like things to be a certain way, so I can't fuss if y'all do, right?"

"No, sir."

Kyler rolled his eyes. She made her momma sound like a mean one. Now, she could be when it came to food, especially if she'd cooked...

And Henley could be fierce, if she was pressed too hard, that was for sure.

"I like all the fixins," he said, laughing at Paige, who was already counting candy.

"I also like all the fixin's," Austin agreed.

"I like just cheese," Dallas explained. "I found a Jolly Rancher for you."

"Ooooh. Trade you." Paige dug out a fun-sized Snickers.

"What do I get, kiddo?" Kyler asked.

"Oh, Daddy. I always give you an Almond Joy."

"My angel girl. You're good to me." He winked at her, and pretty soon, they were pulling into the condo.

"I'm so hungry, Poppy. I love your chili!" Dallas cheered, bouncing in his seat.

"Thanks, kiddo. Come along," Austin added in his snooty butler voice. "Dinner to be served in the living room, sirs and madame."

Paige giggled madly, because now she was in on the joke. "Yay!"

They trooped inside, and Kyler felt so comfortable taking

off his coat and hat, and even kicking off his boots, which he did to preserve the condo's floors, since it was a rental. It surprised him a little, how he was getting used to being at Austin's place.

Coats and hats came off the kids, and they settled on the floor to sort candy.

"Make sure Mr. Mistoffelees doesn't steal your candy. He doesn't need it."

"Is he going to come out this time?" Kyler wasn't sure he'd even seen the kitty, but Paige insisted she had.

"Maybe. But he's so shy," Dallas told him, serious as a heart attack. "He really hides when people come over."

"Maybe he'll come out from under the couch this time." Austin winked at him. "He's a little tuxedo cat, hence the name."

"The name?" He didn't follow.

"Mr. Mistoffelees. It's from TS Eliot and the play *Cats*. That's what he looked like. He was a tuxedo cat."

Kyler liked how Austin didn't make a big deal out of sharing information and didn't make him feel stupid. It was a thing. Just something Austin said.

They scooped up the chili, and he'd been right. It tasted as good as it smelled.

He topped his with onion and cheese and a dollop of sour cream. He also got himself two huge pieces of cornbread. There was precious little finer than cornbread.

Paige got a bit of everything, Dallas had cheese, and Austin got cheese and Fritos.

It was— It was easy. Paige knew where they kept their spoons. Then there were the fancy fizzy waters in cans Austin kept for the kids.

It was a little like being in a family. Kyler was man enough to admit that he liked it.

"So what do you normally do on Halloween?" he asked. "I mean, after the kids go to bed."

"Oh, I used to watch scary movies and have a couple of beers. You know, enough to where I could be a little toasty, but not in any way impaired if something happened where he needed me. But it's kind of lonely, so the last few years I've hung out with people online who were lonely too." Austin winced. "God, that sounds so damn pitiful."

"No. No...well, maybe a little." Kyler kind of got it though. He and Henley had been separated for four years, so he'd only had Paige two of those Halloweens. "Still, I have to tell you, it's not like I was out partying. Most at those times."

"Oh, I imagine you've had some good parties. I'm...I'm kind of staid. You know, I mean I did college, I got my masters. I fell in love. I got married. We had a baby. And then?" Austin shrugged. "It didn't last."

"And he's not?"

Austin shook his head once and said, "No. Not even a sniff, and that wasn't on me. I'm the sperm donor. He wasn't interested in being added to the birth certificate, and he wasn't interested in any of his parental rights if he'd had any. Not an issue."

"Oh." There were some hardcore anger issues there. He got it, but he didn't. He and Henley weren't some huge love match or anything, they were good friends. They'd had sex a couple of times, they got pregnant, they had a baby.

But they talked about Paige daily. Haley paid her child support like clockwork. She saw Paige every time she could. It really was a good break-up, and they were, in their own little way, kind of still a family.

Not even kind of. They *were* a family.

Sort of like he and Austin and the kids were forming a family and—

Oh man, he was wigging himself right the hell out.

Because that sounded terrifying in his brain. They were just friends. Even if he did find himself staring at Austin.

A lot.

Suddenly he realized he'd been in his head for a bit there and Paige was kind of staring at him and Austin was quiet. Dead silent.

Damn it.

"Sorry, man. I got my train derailed."

"It's okay, Daddy," Paige said. "Dallas has his poppy. He doesn't even know the other guy. It's not like me and Mama, where Mama works, and it's best that I live with you, but she still loves me. That's different."

"It is. It's very different. Different families happen all the time."

Austin nodded. "This is true. We choose our families sometimes. That's a good thing. We surround ourselves with people who love us and care about us and want the best for us. That's what a family is."

Dallas beamed at his father, eyes happy, that smile easy. "Daddies and daddies can be family. Mommies and daddies can be family. Mommies and mommies can be families. Sometimes there's one person with a kid with a family. Sometimes there's two people and they're grown-ups and they're a family. And sometimes there's a person and a dog and they're a little family. And then there's grannies and all the other things too."

He could tell Dallas had heard this conversation many times over.

And while many of his cowboy friends would fall over laughing at the very idea, Kyler liked it. "That sounds great, guys. Seriously. I was sad a minute for anyone who wouldn't want to know how cool you are, Dal. Right, Paige?"

"Right! He's an asshole."

"Paige!" He had to work hard not to laugh his ass off.

Dallas's eyes went wide. "You said a cuss!"

"Sorry. I didn't mean to. Much."

"Well, you two keep the cat away and figure out the candy. No more than one piece. Kyler, you want to help with dishes?" Austin asked.

"Sure." Uh-oh. He hoped he wasn't in trouble.

Austin brought him into the kitchen, offered him a smile. "I haven't discouraged Paige from talking about her mom. I think Dallas likes to hear about different family units. She's good to Paige, right?"

"She is. She's not... Well, she's not easy, but she loves her, and she never mistreats her, and she bends over backward to do things with her."

"Excellent. Paige worships her, you can tell. She showed us footage of her racing."

How the hell did Paige know how to do that?

"That's cool." He chuckled. "I get a little worried that she's unhappy, but she never acts like it."

"She's a firecracker. She's going to be wild one day."

"God, yes. I keep trying to keep her reined in but also confident." And it was a full-time job.

"I keep trying to keep him confident, but safe, so I hear you."

He glanced sideways at Austin. "I wasn't freaked out about him having two dads, just FYI."

"Oh, good. Not that he did, but one day, I hope to actually get laid again."

Kyler chuckled, because he heard that. And it was weird how thinking on Austin and getting laid in the same breath seemed natural as all get-out. He would tuck that away for later review. "Yeah, I get that. I've been on a serious not roll."

"Right? It's tough, when you're a single dad."

"It is. Half the folks I meet want to settle down and let me raise more kids without getting to know me, and the other half don't want me to have kids." Kyler raised his eyebrows.

"Hazard of the rodeo, I guess." He wondered if it was the same in the gay Aspen community. Or anywhere for that matter.

"Most everyone I know looks at him and they run. He's amazing, but he's not your average little boy."

"I think he's great." They grinned at each other, and he thought some things never changed. You always yearned for what you didn't have and ignored the challenges it would present.

It was the way of things.

"I'd be happy to watch scary movies with you, post-sugar crash."

"Yeah?" Austin's eyes lit up. "Thanks, man."

"Hey. I love the idea of not having to drive back out while the drunks are out, and I like the company." A lot, in fact. He liked it a lot.

"Well, we'll all have our slumber party, then. It'll be a lovely time. Your critters are all okay?"

"They'll be fine. I fed before I left, and I can head out early." Damn. Okay, cool.

"No, Daddy. We have all our trampolines tomorrow and pizza!"

"I can go get myself showered, changed, and come back here, baby. Like before breakfast. Is that okay?"

"Oh. Yes! I think it's the greatest. It's a special weekend!"

"Yay!" Dallas threw himself down into a handstand.

"Does that work for you, man?" he asked Austin.

"It does! I've got tons of pillows and blankets. Sweats too, if you'd like."

He measured Austin with his eyes. "Yes, that would work. So are we going back out, hooligans? Or are we done?"

"Do you want to go out?"

"We could play games and watch movies in our jammies. Poppy said we could have popcorn and pancakes in the morning."

Paige chewed her lip, then examined her candy. "Okay! We have enough loot!"

"Then I can even put out the candy bowl and turn the lights on in case anyone comes." Austin beamed.

Dallas nodded. "Poppy has candy above the fridge, for if we run out."

"It's for trick-or-treaters, son."

"Uh-huh. We're trick-or-treaters!"

"Never fear, there will be plenty. Come on, kiddo. Let's get cleaned up and changed, huh? Time for Annie to hang up her rifle." He was so damn tickled with the evening he could bust.

And he hadn't had his candy yet.

It had been a wild and woolly Halloween night.

The kids were ramped up on sugar and excitement and 'scary movies'.

And of course, because his light was the only porch light on in the entire damn complex, they'd had at least three million trick-or-treaters.

Possibly more.

So he'd had to send Kyler out to get extra candy, and of course, when Kyler came back, it wasn't just a bag of treats.

It must have been every single thing City Market had on tap.

Possibly City Market and the Walgreens.

It was like a chocolate and hard candy explosion.

Now all the lights were off, and the kids were asleep and drooling in their little makeshift tent in Dallas's bedroom.

They started with *Halloween*, and both of them shared a

beer and a pizza, because chili was great, but scary movies and Butterfingers deserved pizza.

Then they decided to stay old school and watch *A Nightmare on Elm Street*.

They'd heckled and laughed until Kyler had him stop the movie about the point where Johnny Depp was going to get eaten by the bloody bed of doom so that he could go to the bathroom.

So Kyler did, and Austin sort of laid there with his head back on the sofa. Everybody online was gonna wonder where he was, but he wasn't really sure what he was supposed to say.

I'm hanging out with my son's best friend's dad, who is straight and a little wigged-out about me being gay, but that's cool? We're still being cool. Oh, also he's, like, the body double of my best character and...

Yeah, no. He'd just ghost.

He sat there with his eyes closed, trying not to think perverse thoughts about Kyler because he wasn't that kind of guy. He wasn't a creeper.

He thought that Kyler was really hot and sweet and kind and...fascinating.

And that didn't mean anything when push came to shove. Because Kyler was into melons and he was into bananas, which was not even apples and oranges.

He was about to doze off when a change in the air made him open his eyes, and Kyle stood there by the couch, watching him. For a wild moment, he thought he'd awakened in Freddy's nightmare world and that Kyler was going to stab him with knife fingers.

Then Kyler grabbed the blanket he'd left on the couch and sat down next to him again.

He breathed a sigh of relief, which might be premature, he thought, because Kyler cleared his throat.

"So. I picked the wrong door when I was hunting for the bathroom."

"No biggie." He didn't have a secret lair or a dungeon or—

Oh.

Oh, dear.

He did have an office with poster-sized images of his covers framed on the walls...

Fuck a doodle doo.

"Anything you want to tell me, Austin?" Kyler's eyes glittered in the gloom.

"What do you want me to say? I told you I was a writer. You never mentioned you were a cover model. I didn't think you wanted me to bring it up. None of the photos are explicit, and the model release says your image could be used on a gay romance."

"It does." Kyler shrugged. "It's a little weird, huh?"

Shit. He hoped he hadn't ruined his son's friendship. And his. He thought he and Kyler were becoming friends.

"Yeah, but I didn't want to embarrass you. Dallas has zero idea. This isn't going to get out, I swear." He liked Kyler. He didn't want to hurt the man's feelings.

"No, that's fine. I mean, if I was worried about that, I would worry about Koby. That man chitchats."

"Okay. I didn't mention it, because...I didn't know how, and then you didn't say, 'oh, I pose for book covers,' so..."

"Well, no. It's a good gig, and I'm not ashamed of it, but I didn't want to be all, oh you write books? I'm on some."

They stared at each other. "The fans really loved them, you know."

"Yeah?" Kyler's lips curved. "Obviously you did too."

"I'm a healthy gay man, Kyler. Of course I did." He wasn't going to pretend to be straight or blind.

He would swear those cheeks went red, but it was hard to

tell in the flickering light from the TV. "That's very flattering, Austin."

He waited for the "but" where Kyler told him the kids couldn't spend the night anymore or that he was going to get Paige and go home. It didn't come.

"You're okay?" he asked.

"I think so, yeah." Kyler chuckled. "I may be a little more bent than you think."

"I can handle bent. I want you to know that I enjoy this—hanging together." And he loved the idea of bent.

"I love it, man. I haven't had someone to just... be me with in a long time. A long time. You make it easy."

"Thank you. That makes me feel ten thousand feet tall." And that was the truth. He'd felt like he'd forgotten how to be an in-person friend.

"Yeah. Well, I saw what that looks like in your office," Kyler teased.

"You like that, do you? They're great covers. I love them."

"It's a little squirmy, but yeah. I mean, I love the covers."

"Me too. I'm glad you took the job. No one else could be Maverick." And no one else ever would, after this last book was finished.

"Yeah? Thanks. So are there going to be more books?" Kyler asked it casually, but watched him pretty close.

"There's one more. He's been through some stuff, but he's finally getting his absolute happily ever after."

"Nice. Have I done the cover for it already?" Kyler chuckled. "Not that I'm trying to get more work."

"I asked for a winter shot, but I can use what I have, if I need to..." He wanted a shearling coat deal, maybe the curve of Kyler's jaw.

"Well, you let me know. You got an in with the model now."

"Nice." He couldn't stop his grin for love or money.

"Right? Not that I would deny Koby and Tom their cut. They were life savers." Kyler grabbed a Reese's.

"They're amazing. They found me the perfect model."

Kyler beamed at him, and he breathed easier. It was going to be okay.

He was not going to lose his good friend.

That sounded like a treat, not a trick. He grabbed a handful of candy of his own, wincing when someone else met a bloody end.

Halloween seemed so much shinier this year.

Chapter Ten

"Daddy, do I hafta go with Momma this week?"

Kyler glanced at Paige in surprise, eyebrows rising. "You don't want to go?" Henley was due any damn minute. She was taking Paige to Texas to see her folks for Thanksgiving.

"No. I want to have turkey with Dal and play video games."

"Well, we can do that for the next holiday, kiddo. Dal will be here and so will the games. But your momma is almost here." He kept it light and easy.

"Can't Momma stay here this one time? Dal says she can come over..."

"Oh, honey, her momma and daddy want to see you. You don't see Granny and Grampy very often now, huh? They love you so much." He hated to guilt her into things, but dammit, her grandparents needed time with her too.

She sighed. "He'll remember me, though? Right?"

"Of course he will. How about we ask Mr. Austin if he can do a video call while you're gone?" Whew. She was caving.

"Oh. Can you? Would you? I could introduce them to Mommy and Granny and Grampa?"

"I will ask, baby girl. I know how much it means to you to let them meet your friend." He itched to reach out and stroke her hair like he had when she was a baby. She would just duck.

"Okay. Okay, but you're going over, right? Dallas said you could. He said you could spend the night, even."

"I will. And I'll send pictures if you do." He grinned at her, because he could hear Henley's rig driving in.

"Okay. I want to show her my new room and stuff, though?"

"Yes. She's going to want to come in and see the house and maybe go to the barn, kiddo. I bet y'all leave out after supper, and you can sleep." He needed to warn Henley about all the stuff with the new bestie.

"Yeah. I'm going to miss you. You'll call me every day?"

This had never been hard before.

Paige ran for her room, so Kyler headed out onto the big old front porch he'd borrowed from all those long, low Texas ranch houses. The boards were still so new they squeaked.

Henley swung out of her cherry red Ford duallie, her bright blonde hair pulled back in a ponytail. She was wearing a Rangers tee over a long-sleeved shirt, a pair of ancient jeans that loved every curve of her body, and sparkly flip-flops, of course.

Even though it was Thanksgiving and snowing, she was wearing fucking flip-flops.

She always—always—made him smile.

"Lord have mercy this weather," she hollered over. "Did you do this on purpose?"

"I know! It's like, what, ten thousand degrees in Dallas right now?" he shot back.

She winked at him. "Possibly. I had the good Lord to turn

it up so that Mama wouldn't have to cook the turkey inside. She could put it out on the front porch to roast."

He had to grin as Henley ran up and hugged him hard, kissing his cheek.

"I've missed y'all. You look amazing."

"So do you, honey." Henley had been the worst lover on earth, but she was a damn good friend and one hell of a mama.

She grinned, kind of looking around a little, taking it all in, and he swelled with pride.

The house was beautiful, and he knew it. With the snow on the ground, the A-frame was a picture-perfect Colorado log cabin.

"I like the porch. I like it a lot. Where's my girl?"

He chuckled and shook his head. He'd pretend to be disappointed that Henley was more interested in their daughter than the house, but it was a lie. He loved how Henley loved Paige. "She's getting her stuff together. She wants you to see her bedroom."

"She excited to be coming out to the ranch?"

"Well—" He didn't want to have to do this part because it felt weird. Paige had never not wanted to go with Henley. He wasn't even a hundred percent sure now she didn't want to go with Henley.

As it was, she didn't want to miss her new friends.

She blinked at him, those huge fake lashes causing wind. "What's wrong?"

He sighed, shook his head. "She's sort of mad about missing Thanksgiving with her friend Dallas in Dallas. I mean, Dallas isn't in Dallas. Paige will be in Dallas, but Dallas will be here and…yeah."

One perfectly coiffed eyebrow lifted to her forehead. "All right. Well, that's to be expected, I guess. That's gonna get worse. It's good that she has friends."

"Oh, I know, I know." He didn't want Henley to think that he was at fault for any of this, that he was encouraging her to not want to go or something. Shit, he didn't know. "There's so much to talk about."

"So I want to meet this Dallas kid when I come back. He sounds very important. I heard a lot about his father too. Austin?"

Kyler shook his head. "Yeah, Austin's the dad. Dallas is a sweetheart. Kind of a nerdy little boy, but he and Paige get along like a house afire."

"She told me he does gymnastics, and he's really good at it. I told her I'd start paying for gymnastics lessons if she wanted to do it."

Oh, that little shit. He'd told her he couldn't swing it. "Well, that would be a kindness, but you know, you don't have to. She's already swimming and trampolining and 4-H-ing and Girl Scouting."

Henley cracked up. "It's good for her to learn to do things. I think she is a little desperate to be a normal kid for a little while. That's okay." Henley chuckled, the sound low, sure. "She's a rodeo kid, top to bottom. Eventually, she'll be out racing and staying in a trailer and worrying the shit out of both of us."

"Well, she could ride with you for the first twenty years or so of her career. Maybe thirty?"

Henley answered, not a bit of doubt in her voice. "Maybe forty. Well come on, show me the inside of your house. My goddamn toes are freezing."

"You need better boots up here, Texas," he teased. "Come on, and don't you dare give me shit about the kitchen." He was still hanging cabinets and all.

"You ain't Thanksgiving-ing in here are you? You want to come home with us?"

"No. No, I'll go to Austin's." His cheeks heated, and he damned those freaking blood vessels. That was all he needed.

"That's sweet. He's a single dad too, huh?"

"Yeah."

She stared at him, and her lips parted to ask questions he didn't want to answer, when Paige came running in.

"Momma! Momma, I've missed you. Come see my new room! It's as big as a *trailer*!"

"Oh, wow. Then you'll be so comfy." Henley let Paige haul her out of the kitchen.

He went to pour Henley a cup of coffee, heavy on the cream, light on the sugar. He could hear Henley's voice, low and soft, praising Paige.

This was good. This was great. In fact, this gave him a moment to breathe. To try to figure out what he was gonna tell Henley about Austin. Because she was gonna ask. He'd seen it in her eyes. He knew her too damn well.

What was there to tell about Austin? That the guy had his picture up in his office? That he was the star of some kind of fictional fantasy? That he really liked that idea?

Should he tell her that sometimes late at night, when he and Austin were dozing on the couch after the kids had gone to bed and were having a sleepover, he wanted to kiss the guy?

Was that something a guy told his ex? Maybe it was something he should tell *his* ex.

He just didn't know.

But he probably needed to get that straight in his head before he talked to anybody about it. Henley or Paige or Austin or anyone else.

One way or the other, he was more than a little fond of the guy, and spending Thanksgiving with him and his son seemed like a fine idea. Even if Austin called it Friendsgiving.

He still wasn't exactly sure why Austin wasn't taking

Dallas down to New Mexico to spend the holiday there, but he didn't want to ask, either. Family stuff was hard, and if Austin wanted to talk about it, well, he would no doubt explain it all on Thursday.

He was heading over early Thursday after feeding and then coming back for movie night on Friday. He thought Austin was lonely.

He had a feeling he would be too. Maybe he would take an overnight bag in his truck. He could drive to his own place to feed and be back before anyone woke up.

There was an amazing sofa in Austin's office, in fact, and the sectional had three recliners on it. So there was always room for him. And Austin had the softest damn pillows...

Every so often he'd end up in the bathroom upstairs and catch a glimpse of Austin's messy bed through the open door and think totally inappropriate thoughts.

"Why's your face all red?" Henley asked.

Kyler jumped half a foot, and Henley hooted.

"Boo!"

"You are not funny."

"Are you kidding? I'm hilarious. You did a great job on her room. She's really happy."

"Thanks. She picked it out, and I toned it, uh, down." He'd made it a room she could grow into.

"Yeah, she's got a lot of energy, and she's really starting to read a little better. That's amazing."

"It is." School-school was doing her some good. He handed Henley her coffee. "So how are you doing? Do you need anything?"

"Shit, you know me, Ky. I am footloose and fancy-free and good to go."

"Well, I'm glad. Your folks excited?" He was ignoring her hot cheek comment.

"Tickled to death. Momma is going to take her shopping for Christmas. Expect many sparkles."

"I always do. Just no haircuts. She was hysterical last time, and now she's in school."

"No haircuts. You have my word. You promised her she can videochat her boyfriend?"

"Dallas. She's almost six. She has a *friend*."

"Ah. So it's you with the boyfriend?"

"Wha-aa-t?" His voice rose on the word, and he clamped his lips together to keep from babbling.

"You know the dad. What's up with him?" She chuckled, soft as all get out. "Seriously, you are going to spend Thanksgiving with him. Is he cute?"

No. No, he was hot. And Austin was really intense and a bit geeky and fun to hang out with. "Not cute. He's just a dude. He was nice enough to invite me over for Thanksgiving."

"Huh. Okay. Wasn't he going to his family's?"

"I have no idea. That's none of my business."

"Paige says you'll spend time together. That you spent the weekends over there, sometimes coming home here to feed. That's not weird?" She gave him one perfectly arched eyebrow.

"It's not weird. We're two single dads." And he was feeling more than a touch defensive. He kind of needed her to hush up.

"Well, but what do you have in common?"

He blew out a breath, then held up a hand, ticking things off. "Our kids. Our lack of relatives here. Jobs that make it hard to get to know people. Movies. Books."

She squinted. "Paige says he likes hard books."

He rolled his eyes. "Like classics? Yes. But he writes romance novels and calls them mind candy. And he loves Louis L'Amour and Zane Grey."

"And *Lord of the Rings*. Paige was telling me all about *The Hobbit*..."

"Yep." They were all reading it aloud and then they were going to watch the movie. The 1970s animated one first...

"That seems...odd for a little cowgirl."

"Why? It's all heroes and swashbuckling, really." He sighed, scrubbing a hand over his chin. "You got something to say, Henley? Because I feel like I'm walking on eggshells for some reason, and that isn't like us."

"I—no! No, I feel like she's building a life without me. It makes me a little sad, that's all."

"Oh, honey, you're her hero. When you were in the All-American last month, we all sat and watched your every ride, and she told us what you did to be so good. She's just in the first flush of a new thing."

Henley smiled for him, kissed his cheek. "Thanks. I know this is right. I don't want to lose her, you know?"

"I do know." He'd been horrified at the thought that Henley's folks might try to fight him for his baby, but they'd been so generous. And they could come see her anytime. "You're her momma. I wouldn't mess that up. She needs you."

Henley stroked his arm. "She needs stability and friends and Girl Scouts, but I'm glad she's my girl."

He gave her a hug, and for the first time it didn't feel awkward. There was no remnant of chemistry there, nothing but the love for someone who was family. Thank God. This was what he needed to be able to co-parent with her.

Co-parent.

He'd literally just thought co-parent. Wow.

"Okay, so what's for dinner? No turkey. We're going to be inundated with turkey."

He snorted. "No, Paige requested my spaghetti. Apparently your mom doesn't do it right."

Henley cracked up. "No one but *Daddy* does that right."

"You got that shit straight." He was the king of spaghetti sauce, or at least his little girl thought so, and that was really what was important.

He knew it was only four days, but God, he was going to miss her.

Chapter Eleven

"No, Mom." Austin shook his head, even though he knew she couldn't see him through the phone. "You've got your hands full with the daughter and the daughter-in-law fixing to pop off with more babies. Wimberley and I decided just to give you a break."

He didn't mention that Wimberley was spending Thanksgiving in some sort of a weird-assed women's retreat he was fairly sure was a massive lesbian hookup in Sedona.

And also, he was having his cover crush over for the holiday and the weekend.

Really, the only one unhappy about this entire situation was Dallas.

Dallas was pissed.

If he didn't get Paige, he wanted Granny and Grandpa.

He had to be honest, Granny and Grandpa were very busy with upcoming brand-new babies, and that was not going to help the situation one bit.

So.

Home it was.

"I just feel bad. I don't want you to be alone and starving."

"Mom, I'm not going to starve. Even if I didn't order Thanksgiving dinner from a restaurant, which I did, I wouldn't have starved. I know how to make chips and dip. I can make chicken nuggets in every available dinosaur size and shape. And mostly what we're going to have is mashed potatoes and snacks."

And pie.

He'd picked up one pecan, one pumpkin, and one apple. Because he wanted a piece of pecan and pumpkin together with whipped cream, dammit. But Dallas wouldn't eat either one of those, so the apple pie was for him.

Surely between the three of them they could eat pie for breakfast and have lunch and dinner dessert.

It would be fine.

Kyler was bringing... something. Some kind of salad, he thought, and a thing of macaroni and cheese. Apparently the man was the prince of noodle dishes, thanks to Paige.

"I want to see you and Dallas, honey. You know that. I'm not going to forget him in the baby avalanche. What about Christmas?"

"We'll have to see. It depends on all of Dallas's extracurricular stuff."

Mom snorted. "His 'extracurricular stuff'. This is my grandson you're speaking about. What does he do? Competitive reading?"

That sounded fun. "Be nice. He has gymnastics, he has... uh...scouts. He goes and does scouts. Sometimes. When we remember. Oh, and horseback riding. He's learning about horses and trampolining, which is like gymnastics, sort of."

"Have we made you angry? I'm serious. I haven't meant to."

Dammit. That was the last thing he needed—hurt parent.

"No, Mom. No. Dallas has a very good friend, Paige, and she didn't get to stay with her dad this Thanksgiving. So she'll be with her dad for the first half of Christmas break. Or the last. I'm not sure I understand how it's going to work honestly, but Dallas is very intent about staying home and hanging out with her. So I need to figure that out. It's his first real friend."

"Well, okay. That actually makes sense." She chuckled, the sound soft. "Oh, honey, you are a great father. I know sometimes Dallas is challenging."

"No. No, Mom, he's never challenging. He's just mine. But one way or the other, we will see you over the Christmas holidays for sure."

He wasn't gonna tell her even for a second that another reason he wasn't traveling is because he kind of wanted to hang out with Kyler and, he didn't know…spend some time?

So far everything he and Kyler had done involved the kids. Oh, Kyler had spent the night, but they had always been wrangling rambunctious children. Without Paige's energy to keep Dallas ramped up, Austin hoped they would take some actual time getting to know each other.

He sure thought they were friends, but he wanted to maybe be more. That probably wasn't realistic, but it didn't stop his hopeful little heart of hearts from wishing Kyler was watching him like he thought Kyler was watching him. Did that even make sense?

"Maybe your dad and I will come down for a while over Christmas break."

"Sure. I would love that. So would Dallas. He wants to see you."

"I'm excited that he has a friend that he wants to spend time with," Mom said.

"Oh God, Mom. Me too. I swear to God, I thought he was going to never actually connect with someone."

She chuckled. "I worried about that with you too, you know. Books are so much more interesting than other kids."

Dad's voice sounded. "Honey, he's not got his doctorate yet. He's a kindergartener. You have to give him a little time."

God save him from logical parents. "I know, I know. I didn't say it was rational. I just said I worried. He doesn't seem to connect in gymnastics class or at the park. Hell, he and Paige made friends because this bully kept beating him up and breaking his glasses."

"Are you absolutely sure he shouldn't be in Taekwondo or judo or boxing or something? I worry about him getting beat up."

"Don't worry, Paige is a literal cowgirl, and apparently she is not afraid to indulge in fisticuffs."

"Did you just say 'fisticuffs'? In a sentence? On purpose?"

"I did. Don't make me break out even more archaic words."

"I won't." He chuckled at the patently false outrage in his mother's voice.

"I'm so proud of you. Let me talk to my grandson."

"Sure." Relieved, he shut his own damn mouth and called Dal. "Granny is on the phone, kiddo!" He grinned at the sudden stampede of Dallas's feet on the stairs, and he handed over the phone.

"Granny! I miss you."

He went over to check on the delivery for tomorrow's food, keeping an ear out for Dallas. Usually Dal didn't tell tales, but he never knew what might pop out, nonetheless. Pies. Check. Turkey. Yep. Dressing. Woo.

"—going to have a friend over for turkey day. He's very nice and Daddy likes him. They're best friends like me and Paige—"

He tilted his head. Were they? He supposed that, to Dallas, he and Kyler were. Dal couldn't see his online friends, didn't know his old roommate from college. They hung out. They texted. They— Damn. Kyler was his bestie, he guessed.

It was all right with him. He cared for Kyler. Genuinely. If he let himself, in fact, he would get carried away.

"Okay, Granny. I love you, bye."

"Hey don't hang—" He sighed, because Dallas trotted over to hand him his phone.

"Mr. Kyler texted. Do you think that means Paige stayed home?"

Ah, that explained the abrupt disconnect. He checked. The text said *<And she's off>*

"No, son. She's gone to Texas with her momma." *<want to come over early?>*

<God yes> Kyler sent a crying emoji.

<Come on. We'll watch movies and have pizza> "Mr. Kyler is lonely. He's coming over, okay?"

"Okay." Dallas's lip quivered. "Paige is gone, huh?"

"Yep. But she'll be back in a few days."

"I know, Daddy. But it makes me sad."

"Yeah, but she needs to go see her mom, you know? I mean, that's important. She only gets to see her mama every so often. And this is super special."

As soon as he said it, he knew it was a mistake. Dallas was already wigged.

"I don't have a mama. And nobody cares."

"You're right, you don't." Austin knew this was going to be a problem at some point. He did. Being nontraditional in any way was always going to be an issue.

"Why not? Why don't I have a mama? It's because you're gay, right?"

Austin nodded, refusing to seem unsure in this situation. He had wanted to be a father. He had become one. "Yep, that's exactly why. I hired a lady—this really, really neat lady, by the way—to grow you in her tummy because I wanted to be a daddy so bad, and I wanted you."

"Was I supposed to have another dad too?" He could see Dallas's little wheels twirling in his brain.

Every so often it would be nice to have a less precocious child. Not all the time, mind you, but every now and again it would be nice.

"You were. I was married when we got pregnant. But he decided that he didn't want to be a dad."

"He didn't like me?"

Austin shook his head. "It had nothing to do with you, baby. He didn't even know you."

He had been scared of being a dad. Christopher had been terrified of the idea of being a special needs father, and he was kind of a selfish asshole. No amount of being good in bed could fix that. "What matters is that I loved you from the second I saw you. You're my kid. You're—amazing." He felt his eyes get hot and achy with the need to cry, so he calmed himself down.

He didn't want Dallas to be overwhelmed by emotions he wasn't ready to understand at six.

Austin didn't understand half the emotions this little boy brought out in him—this wealth of love and need to protect and this incredible pride.

Not to mention terror. Sheer fucking terror that he could screw this up.

There ought to be a good handbook on how to be a single dad.

All the ones he'd read were basically made for straight dudes or queer couples and—

"I think having a mom would be cool."

"Yeah?" They moved to sit on the sofa, side by side, Dallas so serious.

"Yeah. I mean. Moms make cookies and brownies for bake sales, and they like flowers. Sometimes they're Superwoman. And they get earrings."

"'Earrings'." Well, that was unexpected.

"Uh-huh. I see it on the TV. The daddies bring the mamas earrings, sparkly ones, and the mamas go 'ohh', and it's really cool."

"Well, I guess I could have an earring, but...I don't know. I don't know that I'm the earring kind."

Dallas shook his head. "There's already an earring kind. That's a mom. You're not a mom. You write books and make chicken nuggets and take me to trampoline. Also, I think I kind of need you and not a mom because I have nightmares, and you make them go away."

That little face wore such a serious expression. He didn't dare smile.

"Well, I don't intend to go anywhere, so we're good."

This was the strangest discussion, but so wonderful. He loved to talk to his son. The way Dallas's kid brain worked fascinated the hell out of him.

"Paige's mom doesn't live with them, though, so that's kind of like us."

"Mmmhmm. And Kyler has to work hard to be a single dad."

"I like him." Dallas leaned against him. "So do you."

"I do. He's a nice man, and he's good to kids and animals."

"Mmmhmm. And he smiles at you. I like that."

He had no idea what that one meant, so he let it go.

"Okay, then. It's a few sleeps and then Paige will be home, and Mr. Kyler will be here to hang out. Fair enough?"

"Yep." Dallas grinned. "And there will pie and Granny said she would call again tomorrow."

Whew. Seemed like the crisis was averted some.

Thank God. He got it. He did. It didn't matter. Dallas needed to deal.

<*On my way*> Wow. Kyler must have been bored if he'd already bedded down the animals for the day.

<K. Pick up some cocks at the store? I ran out>
<What?>

He read his last text. *<COKES. COKES! OMG>*

He got a laughing to tears emoji. *<OK>*

Oh, God. He was a moron. He cackled, shook his head, and Dallas blinked at him.

"What's funny, Poppy?"

"Oh, I made a silly typo. Do you want pizza or a little spaghetti and bread?"

"Mr. Kyler makes better sauce than the restaurant, Daddy. I'll have pizza."

"Okay. I'll order pizzas. Play your game, and Mr. Kyler will be here soon, all right?"

"Okay, Daddy." Dallas beamed, and he went to make the food call. "Cheese?"

"Can we have pepperoni-onis?"

"Of course we can!" Apparently Paige had changed Dal's mindset on pepperonis.

"Cool!" Dallas did a little butt wiggle dance. God, he loved that kid.

He washed up while Dallas played, but stopped short of putting on any kind of cologne. Dallas would be sure to mention it, even if Kyler didn't notice, and how embarrassing would that be?

Kyler arrived about the same time as the pizza, smiling and holding up a bag. "I got the drinks."

"Oh, smart man, not having to say that danger word."

"I about stopped breathing I was laughing so hard." He followed Austin into the condo. "How's it going?"

"Better. He talked to his granny, and that made him happier."

"Yeah. Paige was having a tough time going, but then her gran called and told her how excited she was to see Paige and her mom, and they were off and running."

"Excellent. Dallas is excited to be able to keep you safe and comfy."

"Yeah? Well, that's cool." Kyler winked at him. "I also got us some of that cheese ball and some crackers for later."

"Excellent. I ordered pizza. It's a pre-Thanksgiving tradition. One meat, one pepperoni."

"Hey, I like being included in the tradition." Kyler unloaded the Cokes once he got to the kitchen, then put the cheese ball in the refrigerator.

"Are you missing out on any family traditions to be here?"

Kyler turned and leaned against the counter with his butt up against it, his arms straight behind him to prop him up. "Not really. When I was a kid we had some great traditions, but there's really not a whole lot of that left."

"What was your favorite thing?" Austin asked.

"I think probably the football game after the meal. I ended up with a lot of family houses to eat at, some of those folks were not the best cooks."

"No? I hope it's okay that I ordered some of the stuff." He'd been fretting about the idea for days.

"Austin, I'm not gonna yell about anything. I'm pretty happy with about any kind of food as long as it tastes good. We could have had Chinese food for all I care."

"That's an interesting idea, but I think that's more New York than it is Aspen." Even the Chinese places in the Roaring Fork closed for the holidays.

"Yeah, you're probably right."

"So what else did you bring? I didn't see a mac and cheese casserole."

"Yeah, that's because I sent it with Henley and Paige. Paige made the big teary eyes for me, but I brought all the stuff to make another one for you guys. I'll do it tonight before we go to bed so it can sit in the fridge till tomorrow."

"Hey, you didn't have to do that. I mean I'm glad you did

because Dallas is desperately curious to see what your mac and cheese tastes like. I asked him if he wanted spaghetti and meatballs from the pizza place, and he said your sauce was better." Which shocked him, because that kid loved noodles.

Kyler beamed. "I'm glad he thinks so. I know Paige likes it too. It's one of the few recipes I got from my family that's worth it."

"My mom's always done a huge thing. Always." And Austin had all this guilt.

Kyler rolled his head on his shoulders. "Do you mind me asking why you didn't go?"

Austin kind of leaned forward a little bit, making sure Dallas was still occupied. "I'm sort of desperate to talk about it, to be honest."

Kyler handed him a Coke. "Spill, man."

Oh, thank God. He opened his Coke and started talking. "You know, I have this big family, right? Three brother—well, one brother, two sisters. I mean, there's four of us."

He stopped and rolled his eyes at himself. "Now, my brother's wife is fixing to pop, and my sister is also pregnant and having troubles. They both live close enough and have kids and need help."

"Okay. Also, yay new nephews?"

"Nieces. Now, add this baby situation to my sister, who, like me, is gay. She decided that she was going to this retreat in Sedona with other women who do things that grown-ups do." He waggled his eyebrows, and Kyler damn near choked on his Coke. "And so she wasn't going to come, so I thought, you know, my mom is super stressed out with these babies coming and all this stuff. Honestly, there's no reason for me to go and make her cook all this food when Dallas and I would really be the only ones there eating. We could just... not and sort of let it be something peaceful for her too, maybe. But I tell you what." He rolled his eyes again, leaning back on the counter of his teeny tiny kitchen. "She is stressed out about this being the first year she isn't making Thanksgiving dinner. My sister—the one who's not pregnant, Wimberley—she's having this big meal delivered that's a huge variety so Mom can eat whatever and so can Dad."

Austin did appreciate that Kyler wasn't acting like he was losing his mind.

"Nobody has to stress—which I think is very kind—and it's a four-hour drive, and there's nobody who will want to play with Dallas and—"

He blew out a huff of hot air, rolled his eyes, and pursed his lips. "Tell me I'm not a terrible son."

"You're not. Parents have to accept that things change too. It sucks on both sides, I think." Kyler gave him a wry smile. "Henley was freaking out because Paige didn't really want to go with her for the first time."

"Oh, man, was she digging in?" Austin thought that could be a sticky problem.

"She was dragging her feet more like. She never wants to be rude, and she does love her momma, but she wanted her first holiday with you and me and Dal here."

"Ouch." He winced. "Is Henley at least glad she has a friend?"

"Tickled as a pig in shit. But she's also worried she's already becoming obsolete, you know?" Kyler popped the top on a Coke too.

"Would you rather have gone?" Austin kind of held his breath.

Now Kyler burst out with a duck noise laugh. "To Henley's folks? God no. I mean, they were always very kind to me, but the day her momma met me, she pulled me aside and told me, 'Son, you'll never be as shiny and bright as the rodeo, and you'll never be as famous as my girl. You aren't going to last a year.' I lasted almost two."

Austin blinked. "Wow. That's— Wow."

"Hey, she was right." Kyler clinked their cans together. "But even without my kid I would much rather be here with friends."

"Well, we're tickled that you're here. I like hanging out, and we can be boys. Dallas informed me."

"Ah. I bet he doesn't mean we get to spit and fart."

He hooted. "Probably not."

Chapter Twelve

Kyler was gonna pop, he was so full. His belly was so tight he felt like a snake who had swallowed something way too big for it. He was surprised at how good the turkey was for being bought and not done in a smoker or deep fryer or something. This whole holiday thing was really good and he was super sleepy now.

He and Austin were sitting on the couch while Dallas sprawled on the floor reading a book, feet up in the air behind him. It was surprisingly quiet and peaceful, which Thanksgivings in his experience had never been before. and Kyler was pretty much in love with the whole idea.

Austin glanced over at him smiling. "You're grinning."

"Am I? I guess so. I'm having a good day."

That smile widened. "I'm glad. We're having a great day too, aren't we, kiddo?"

"Uh-huh." Dallas glanced up. "It's been yummy and fun, but when are we gonna have pie?"

Kyler groaned. "Oh my God, you guys can have pie whenever you want, but I think I'll probably wait for a couple of hours."

"I think we will too. You're rocking back and forth on your belly, kiddo. That's how full you are."

Kyler was chuckling when his phone rang, and he checked it, knowing he had to answer because it was Paige. "Hello?"

"Hi, Daddy. I wanna come home."

Crap. That was never a good way to start a conversation. "Are you not having a good time, baby girl?"

"I miss you, Daddy, and I miss my room, and I miss Dallas, and I wanna come home." She sounded so put-upon.

"Oh, sweetie, don't tell that to your mother."

"I *won't*. That doesn't mean I don't wanna come home." Now she sounded so hopeful, and he knew he was gonna have to dash those hopes. She only had to stay there a couple more days.

"I'm sorry, baby girl, you know I told your mom you would stay until Monday."

Her tone changed to a stage whisper. "Daddy, Momma and Granny are fighting."

"Are they? Are they really, or are they more having heated discussion?" This was Texas Paige was talking about, after all. Heated discussions over Thanksgiving were all the rage.

"They're arguing about everything, including what we're gonna do tomorrow."

"And what do you want to do tomorrow?"

"I want to go shopping. If I'm gonna have to stay here, I want to try to get a Christmas present for Mr. Austin and for Dallas."

He chuckled again. "Not for me?"

"Daddy, you know that I wouldn't leave you out." Her tiny sigh told him he'd stepped in it.

He glanced at Austin who was making faces, waggling his eyebrows, and Kyler pointed his finger at the guy to hush him up, because he wanted to laugh. "I know you're always good to me baby."

"Can I come home then?"

"No, and you can't tell your mom you wanna come home, either. But I tell you what. We'll ask her to come to our house for Christmas instead of you going to Granny's."

"Promise?"

"I do. Now who knows what Momma's going to say to that, but I promise I'll ask."

"Okay, Daddy"

After that the conversation devolved into what did you eat for dinner and what stores are you looking forward to going to that you don't have up here, that sort of thing. She talked to Dallas, too.

After about ten minutes she finally stopped asking to come home and said, "I love you, Daddy. I'll see you soon."

"I love you too, baby, you be good."

He hung up feeling like the worst dad ever but also like he had been the best ex-husband he could be.

"It's hard to be the dad. It's a pain in the butt to be the reasonable one. I wanted to be the fun dad. but since I'm the only one, I can't."

Dallas rolled his eyes at Austin. "You're fun. We just have fun in different ways. Some guys are football dads. Some dads are baseball dads. Some are weightlifting dads. Some dads are comedian dads. You're a writer dad."

"Oh, okay, I'll take that and also trampoline dad."

Kyler nodded. "And he's a gymnastics dad."

Dallas was sort of amazing there.

"He so is. He's also a coffee dad. And a movie dad. Sometimes he's a video game dad. Those are cool dads."

Austin glanced over at Kyler. "I'm a cool dad, see? Mr. Kyler is a cowboy dad and a horse dad."

Dallas nodded, so emphatic. "And a dog dad, and we don't have a dog, Poppy. That's a point off for you."

Austin shot back with, "We can barely take care of the cat. I'm not even sure Mr. Kyler's ever seen the cat."

That wasn't true. That was an exaggeration, and he knew Austin knew it. But part of Austin's job was to exaggerate a little bit.

"He's met Mr. Mistoffelees." Dallas rolled his eyes. "He's just not very friendly. Like me."

Austin's mouth literally dropped open. "You're friendly. Paige is your friend."

"Even Paige says that I'm not friendly. I'm a good friend. There's a difference, Poppy." Dallas was serious as a heart attack. "Friendly is like...always going to see somebody that you don't even know and shaking their hand and saying 'Hi, I'm Dallas. Let's be friends'."

"Now, son, you're just a little—"

"Poppy." Dallas stared at his father like he had grown two heads. "Paige is friendly. I am a good friend. I love my friends, and I take care of them, and I ask for chocolate cupcakes in my lunch even though I don't like them because she likes them and her daddy doesn't buy them for her."

Ouch.

"Good friends like me share their books and their puzzles. And when Paige wants to play dolls, they play dolls."

Austin tilted his head. "You know it's cool if you wanted to play dolls, right?"

"I know. Sometimes I do. Sometimes I don't. That's not the point. The point is if you're a good friend, and your good friend wants to play dolls, you play dolls. And then afterward, maybe she'll play Sherlock. Like that."

Kyler sort of sat and watched. This was like a weird tennis match or something.

Paige was...not quite as complex as Dallas in some ways. And yet in other ways she was so much more mature. So much more savvy, he guessed.

Dallas was very precise.

"Sherlock is good, huh?" Austin grinned at his son.

"Uh-huh. Can I have pie?"

"If you want pie, son, you can totally have pie. Pumpkin?"

"Poppy! I don't like that one!"

"No?"

He could tell this was a regular tease. Austin was hiding a grin for all he was worth.

"No. I want apple, please."

Ah. He'd wondered why there were three kinds of pie. Clearly Dal didn't do pumpkin or pecan. His favorite was pecan. He also knew how to make his ex-mother-in-law's chocolate pie.

"Of course. Whipped cream or ice cream?"

"Squirty cream?" Those were hopeful eyes.

"Of course, son." Austin levered himself up off the sofa. "One slice of pie, coming up."

Austin's ass was right there, close enough to touch.

He wanted to touch it.

What the heck was that? He'd had thoughts about Austin before, but nothing that...specific.

"Can I help?" He stood fast enough to whack them together.

"S-sure!" Austin grabbed him, swaying dangerously.

"Hey. Whoa." He held Austin up, his breath catching as he stared into Austin's eyes, which was weird, because he had to look up.

He never had to look up.

Austin's eyes were like a storm, gray clouds rolling in. He couldn't bring himself to glance away, desperate to know what happened next.

Austin's lips parted, and the fine son of a bitch leaned in...

"Poppy! Pie!"

"Right." Austin pushed off his chest. "Come on, buddy. I'll get you pie. You want whipped cream?"

"Poppy! I said spray cream! Did you forget already?"

"I must have! I'm getting old, huh?" Austin was pink-cheeked and heading for the kitchen.

"No. You're just silly." Dallas followed his dad to the kitchen, which gave Kyler a moment to breathe. And to thump his dick with his middle finger, willing it to go down.

"What the hell was that?" he murmured to himself. He would swear Austin had been about to kiss him, and he'd been damn sure about to kiss the man back. Whew. That was hotter than a two-dollar pistol, and he would have to unpack that when he went to do the feeding, and he could talk to the horses and the air.

Right now, he needed to breathe, to focus on something other than…Austin's eyes.

Maybe he was in a pie sort of space. Pecan pie might render him comatose and he could nap it off.

"Did you want anything?"

"A piece of pecan?"

"Sure. Whipped cream?"

He shook his head. "Nope. I think I'm going to have to change into a pair of sweats, though."

"Sounds like a plan." Austin offered him a quick grin. "I might have to do the same here in a minute."

"No shit on that. I mean, shoot, I mean…" *Dammit*.

Dallas rolled his eyes. "Don't worry, Mr. Kyler. My poppy cusses all the time. I just know to ee-nore it."

"Ignore."

"That's what I said. I ee-nore your cusses." Dallas grinned. "All of them. Even the super bad ones."

"Thank you, son. You're a tiny ray of sunshine." Austin sighed, so dramatic. "Go change. I'm going to finish making him his pie and make sure he doesn't spread it all over the earth or the cat or let the cat steal it or—"

"Poppy!"

Kyler headed back to the teeny office and shut the door, grabbing his bag with his baggiest sweats. God knew his jeans weren't getting any looser, and he wasn't going to ponder the whys of that. It had nothing to do with gaining weight.

He kicked off his boots, sitting in the desk chair to do so. Austin's office was wild, this big converted walk-in pantry filled with books of all sorts, including a big old stack of his own. The walls were painted in a dark brown, and the desk seemed like a monster of a thing, bigger than the space needed, but there were papers and index cards and sticky notes and stacks of papers and reference-type things all over it. It was actually kind of cool—like Austin had curated the room to scream *author*.

The weirdest part about the whole thing were the pictures covering the walls. There were five framed posters, great big old things of him. All with titles emblazoned on them.

Maverick's Choice.
Maverick's Dilemma.
Maverick's Call.
Maverick's Home.
Maverick's Man.

All with his damn body on them.

It was weird, because he'd never really felt hot before, but seeing these? Even all photoshopped and color-corrected. No freckles, no moles, no scars even—and God knew he had those —he was kind of sexy.

And that was weird.

He stood up, put on his sweats, and walked over to the one closest to the door—*Maverick's Man*.

Emblazoned across the poster were five gold stars and then

this quote in italics: *Austin Williams' Maverick is the hottest hero in gay romance.*

Man, he wanted to read these books.

There was no way he was going to ask to read these books.

There was no way he could get caught reading these books.

He had a phone though. Then if he got one of them e-books or an audio book or something...

Nobody would know he was reading these books.

It wasn't even that he was all that interested in some hot boy-on-boy action. Although he kind of was.

God, he really was.

Mostly he wanted to know what was going on in Austin's brain.

He pulled on his sweats. Was Austin confusing him with a book character, or was he using Kyler for inspiration now or what? Was that weird? Was it hot? He wasn't sure.

He wasn't used to being confused and worried. He wasn't used to all of this. He wanted—

He wanted to find out what Austin tasted like, though. He really did. He was going to let that side of himself out, explore it a little. Maybe a lot.

Now he had to figure out how he was going to go about it.

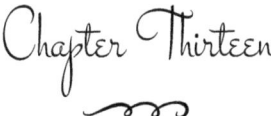

Chapter Thirteen

Austin stood in the toy store. Staring. He had to get toys for Dallas. That wasn't too hard. In fact, he felt comfortable with that, for the most part. Dallas liked mysteries and board games. Anything with cards and stuffed dogs. And puzzles. Austin was easy.

Then he had to buy toys for Paige. Because Paige was Dallas's best friend, and Kyler was Austin's cover model. Or something. But Paige was also not too hard. Breyer horses. He was going to start a collection for her. It seemed reasonable and fun, and they would start with the one closest to the horse he had met at Kyler's. It was apparently not the one Dallas had ridden, but it was the one Paige raced with.

Those two weren't the problem. The kids were easy.

What Austin didn't understand was how his uptight, friendless, never-get-invited-to-the-birthday-party child had become the kid who was invited to every goddamned Christmas party on earth.

There was one at the gym, there was one at the trampoline park. There was one for school. There was one for whatever. There was an invitation to a another kid's house. He was fairly sure Paige had something to do with that. And he wasn't unhappy about it.

It was just that there were now tons of white elephant gifts and things that you had to do and he was very stressed out by this whole situation, because he was an uptight, never leave the house author.

And that made him whiny. That really wasn't why he was feeling so whiny. To be honest, he was feeling out of sorts because Kyler was acting weird. Ever since Thanksgiving, there had been this strange distance between them. And he hadn't done anything wrong.

Had he thought about kissing the man like, whoa, sure, okay. Had he done it? No, no, because consent was important. He couldn't go out and just kiss somebody who was straight. So he hadn't.

Still, he wasn't quite sure what he *had* done. So he wasn't quite sure what to apologize for. He wasn't one hundred percent sure he was supposed to.

Maybe it was a busy time of year. Kyler surely did Christmas things with leather working right? And Austin had deadlines. Kyler had his ex coming. He and Dallas were expecting a visit from Mom and Dad at some point, or at least one of them.

But he missed the easy camaraderie he and Kyler had shared since the beginning of the school year. He missed seeing Kyler sacked out on his couch. All in all, he wished he could go back and change whatever had happened.

He was in the middle of surfing the aisles for Barbie clothes for a December birthday party when his phone buzzed.

<*Is Austin going to Amelia's birthday party?*>
<*Is that the Barbie invitation?*>
<*Yes. What are you getting her?*>
Well, at least Kyler was texting him, right?
<*Call?*>

<Sure> The phone rang, and he hit the answer button. "Hey."

"Hey. What the heck is a Water Rhapsody Barbie?"

"Dude, you have the girl! How do you not know?" He looked up the doll. Huh.

"Because up until this week, she thought those dolls were stoopid, two oos in the middle." The irony lay heavy in Kyler's voice.

"Does that mean I should put her Breyer horses back?" He couldn't help but smile.

"No. She still doesn't want any more of them for herself. The dolls I mean. She says she can play them with Amelia sometimes. She'd still rather visit Dal."

"Okay, so, what do I buy for this party? And what about all the damn Christmas parties?"

"You're at the toy store?" Kyler sounded surprised.

"I'm at the toy store. Why?"

The bell above the door rang. "Turn around."

He did, and there was Kyler. "Dude!"

Kyler tucked his phone away. "Hey. Imagine meeting you here." Kyler grinned, coming to stand next to him. "So, what the hell do we do with all these parties? I'm at a loss too."

"I don't know. I'm a new school dad as well. We have the gym, the trampoline park, the school..." It was overwhelming.

"Yeah, and Paige and I have the Roaring Fork Rodeo Association too. It's nuts." Kyler scrubbed a hand over his face, which was stubbly.

"Yeah. I have a bunch of shit to send to different fans and friends. I'm not thinking about that right now." He winked and grinned.

That seemed to catch Kyler's attention. "Yeah? What kind of stuff do you send?"

"It depends on the friend. My super fans are getting signed posters and keychains this year."

One of Kyler's eyebrows shot up. "Posters of me?"

"Posters of the cover of *Maverick's Home*."

"Oh. But I mean, that is me." Kyler's cheeks went pink.

"No one but me knows that, though. I would never *ever* out you to anyone." Never.

"No, I get that. I do." Kyler gave him an odd glance. "I trust you."

"So can we be buds again, man? Please?"

"Huh? We have been."

"No, you've been avoiding me."

Kyler sighed. "Maybe. I was reading your books, and deciding that I'm on the covers, but that's not me."

"No. Those books were written before I found you, and the series is completely done."

"Is it? That's a bummer. They're good." Kyler chuckled. "Really good."

His cheeks heated, and he couldn't fight his blush. "Yeah? Thanks. I appreciate it. Do you want to go get a coffee after I check out?"

"I do. Please." Kyler grinned. "Buddies again?"

"Buddies again. Yes. We'll need each other to get through Christmas."

"We will." Kyler turned back to the toys. "Barbie."

"Yes. Barbies. I'm like an expert." He rolled his eyes.

"So lay it on me. What do we get?" Kyler bumped shoulders with him.

"I'm thinking clothes. Clothes are always safe and easy. I found two horses for Paige—one from me and one from Dallas, plus a couple of early reader horse books."

"Yeah. Dallas is easy. Books." Kyler grinned. "Okay, this appears to me like it goes with the doll Paige said she wanted, right? Her parents are bound to be getting her that."

"I'm assuming so. God, I hope so. Can you imagine the drama?"

"No." Kyler shuddered. They bought Barbie clothes and some cute gift bags before heading out to have coffee. It felt nice to have some adult time. The kids were in school for another three hours, and he could so have a nice cup of joe, spend a bit of time with Kyler.

They settled in across from each other after they ordered coffees and pastry and a sandwich to share, Kyler grinning at him. "This feels like playing hooky, huh?"

"It so does." So much of their time together revolved around the kids, or existed in that weird late-night space after the children went to bed and Kyler watched movies with him. "I should be writing, but I just haven't been inspired. I'm in my saggy middle stage."

"So what are you writing, if Maverick is done?" Kyler folded his arms on the table and leaned in.

"I'm trying my hand at a set of novels based on a ranch. Maverick was amazing—but he'd solved a bunch of crimes and had a ton of sex. I'm thinking working cowboys." It was a change, but it wasn't romantasy.

"Yeah? Well, you know if you need to come do research, I have the space."

"Yeah? I'd love that. I was worried that I'd done something to you." And it had made him a touch crazy.

"No. No, I got busy with commissions, and I got in my own head a little, but we're good. I promise."

Austin couldn't miss the warmth in Kyler's gaze. "Okay. Cool. I'm tickled you're the image of Maverick, but Kyler is my friend."

Kyler tilted his head, then nodded. "I am. I want that, man."

He huffed out a laugh, relief overwhelming for a relationship with a straight guy. "Me too."

"Cool. I like you, Austin." Kyler took a deep breath. "I also dig you."

His head tilted. "I—"

Did that mean something else to straight guys?

Kyler reached out to touch his hand. "I don't have to do anything about it, but I figured it was only fair to tell you."

Suddenly the truth dawned on him. "You—You're bi?"

"I am, yeah. I mean, I always knew it, but I've never acted on it. Like until now. I guess I am." Kyler's cheeks went bright red. He had a feeling this was the first time Kyler had ever said it out loud.

"Oh. Well then, it feels less creepy to think about you."

"Yeah?" Kyler's grin widened. "You think about me?"

"I'm a healthy man with a gorgeous man next to me, I write romance novels about cowboys, and I like you, Kyler." He rolled his eyes. "I think. A lot."

"Okay. So we can work with that." Kyler chuckled. "Whew. I was worried."

"Next time, just talk to me. I'm not an asshole. I swear." He wasn't a hero, but he was a decent guy.

"I will. I promise. I mean, I try to be an adult and stuff, but my track record with friends and or lovers is bad."

"My ex saw Dallas and ran, right? I hear you."

"That's so crazy. He's an amazing kid, and being a dad is like..." Kyler waved his free hand, the one not holding Austin's. "So damn cool."

"Yes." Simple as that. It stunned him, how much he loved Dallas.

"I get that, at least. I mean, you know I understand the kid thing." Was Kyler really making a case for himself as a potential date?

Austin wasn't sure exactly what he thought about this.

His dick, on the other hand, knew exactly what it wanted.

His body wanted to be up close and personal with Kyler's, and not worry about this or that or relationships or community or shared interests.

Kyler leaned back to sip his coffee. "So what are you guys up to tonight?"

"It's Friday, right?" He thought it was Friday. It felt like a Friday.

"It is, yeah. And no parties until Sunday."

"Would...the trampoline park is closed tomorrow for an 'event'." He made sarcastic, now-I-have-to-deal-with-my-disappointed-son air quotes. "Maybe we could...hang?"

Did that sound too much like he was asking to come and stay at Kyler's?

"You want to come out to my place? The house is pretty damn solid now, and if the weather is good we could have a riding lesson tomorrow or whatever the kids want to do..."

"Yeah? That sounds great. Do your horses like the snow?"

"They do. I've got a couple of shaggy older geldings in right now who think it's the best thing ever."

Ah, that meant Paige's horse didn't care for it.

"That's cool. What would you like me to bring, food-wise?" He could stop and pick up food from anywhere.

"Oh, something warm? Maybe soup? They have some good ones at the City Market. We can make grilled cheese."

"Oh, perfect. Two potatoes and a chicken noodle?" Plus a six-pack for them to share, maybe a cheese ball...

They did love a late-night cheese and beer fest.

What did it say that he knew that Kyler liked port wine or jalapeno and cheddar better than he did the green onion and almond cheese ball, but he didn't know the man's middle name or favorite color?

"What's your middle name, man?"

"Huh?" Kyler blinked at the change of subject, he thought. "Uh, Justin. Kyler Justin Hale. What's yours?"

"Austin James Williams. I was an AJ growing up." It had been easy as breathing, really. Austin was his pseudonym, in a lot of ways.

"Yeah? Huh. My people all call me Ky, unless I'm being scolded." Kyler seemed so pleased, the little information-sharing putting a happy expression in his eyes.

"Ky? Oh, I like that. I like that a lot."

"So...do you like AJ?"

He wanted to know what Kyler wanted to call him. Sort of desperately. "I'm easy."

"I like AJ. It sounds less like what you do and more like who you are."

"Well, then you can call me AJ, and I'll call you Ky. Fair?"

"Sounds grand, honey." Kyler squeezed his hand, then let go to grab a pastry. Oh right. They had food.

Honey.

Okay.

Okay, he could be into that. He really could. It probably only seemed sudden to him. He felt like Kyler had been thinking hard about all sorts of things while he'd worried.

Good old internal dialogue. He got that. He was the king of it.

So why did it surprise him when other people had it?

"What are you grinning about?" Ky asked, a gleam of humor in his eyes.

"I was thinking about...thinking?" His cheeks heated, but it was true.

"Hmmm. Have some sandwich." Kyler pushed the plate toward him. "Better than thinking too hard."

"I was more thinking about you thinking, but yeah. Thinking is hard."

Kyler blinked at him, then his head tilted. "Are all authors like you?"

"Writers, and yes."

"What?"

"I'm not an author. I'm a writer. A storyteller. I want to write stories that make people happy."

"And an author doesn't do that?" Ky was blinking harder.

"I have no idea, but I know they're way more intense than I am." He wasn't changing the world with his keyboard. He was simply adding a little joy.

"Ah. Okay, so an author is like, all literary?"

"Yeah." He winked.

"Got it." Ky gave him a blatant ogling. "I like writers, I think."

"I hope so." So did he, when it came right down to it. He liked a lot of them, but he fantasized about cowboys.

Chapter Fourteen

Kyler grabbed Paige at school, then headed home to make sure the house was relatively clean. He was tickled to have Austin—AJ—and Dallas coming out. They'd really worked hard, the two of them, on making the house comfy, and Paige had insisted on a making a space for books and puzzles for Dal.

"I like having a space for Dal's things. It feels like I have a brother," she announced.

And he'd made the space. God help him.

"Daddy, did you get the Barbie?"

"No, I got clothes for the Barbie. Someone in her family is bound to get her the doll, baby, and it would be rude to make them feel bad."

"Oh. Oh, you think that's how it works? What did Dal get her?"

"Barbie shoes and a little Barbie dressing table to go with her fashion box." Lord, he'd had a crash course in dolls for girls too old for baby dolls.

Paige blinked at him. "You know about Barbies?"

"Yep." Not even a little.

"You do not. You are a boy!"

He rolled his eyes. "Boys can like Barbies."

"Do you like Barbies?" she shot back.

"Well, no…"

"Dal doesn't either."

"But he plays dolls with you sometimes."

"Uh-huh. So I will play detective with him. Though I like that game."

"Oh, I found that Disney Sherlock movie."

Her eyes went wide. "The mouse one? Daddy! That's too cool!"

Bingo.

"Yeah. We can watch it tonight since they're coming to stay over."

"Oh, yay! Are we going to watch Christmas cartoons too? Is Momma coming to stay for Christmas, too?"

"Momma is going to try, baby girl. It's a hard time of year, but she says she wants to." He'd learned to hedge his bets. Henley did her damnedest to keep her promises. She was no flake. But living mostly on the road meant she had some stuff crop up she couldn't foresee.

"She says she'll be here after the finals. She says she'll bring her trailer, so that Dallas can meet her horses."

"See?" Lord. Henley did talk some. "Are you excited for Christmas?"

"I'm excited for Christmas break!" she beamed at him. "We're going to have the most fun in our house!"

"We are." They would make cookies and put up a tree and do all sorts of shit they'd never had a place to do.

"Do you think Santa will come? Dallas says he will. That he'll leave a note with our address." Paige's eyes were lit up, that worry and belief warring with each other. "You promise he'll find us?"

"I swear to God, baby girl. Santa will come." He reached

out to ruffle her hair. "He has a list and his elves check it all the time when people move. Heck, he used to find you on the road."

"He did, and I didn't have Dal to check up on me. Okay, I'm going to believe. What's for supper? Can we make a thousand cookies? Can we get puppies?"

"Puppies? Do you think you might be too busy?" Not that he wasn't hunting for a dog that might need a home now that he was around so much more. One that could hang with him in his workshop...

"Daddy." She rolled her eyes and all of the sudden she was Henley. "No one is too busy for puppies. Not even Dal."

"No? What does Dal want in the way of a dog?" They had a cat, AJ and Dallas. He would bet a dog would have to wait.

"Oh, Daddy. Dallas wants a big dog. He's asking Santa for a hunky. He wants to take it fast-skiing with us."

"A hun—oh, a husky?" He grinned. "That's a lot of dog, kiddo."

"Yes. They make alarm sounds. We saw them on a video. That way if we crash, you can find us." She sounded so *sure*.

Silly, brilliant, creative girl—he adored her.

"True. But a Border collie or a cattle dog could find you and dig you out."

"Or a Saint Bernie could come save me and give me stuff out of his little barrel."

He didn't have the heart to tell her those barrels were an urban legend. He sure as hell didn't want to start in with her on what an urban legend was. So he just let it go.

"What's for supper?"

"Mr. Austin is getting soup, and we're making grilled cheese."

"Oh, I like grilled cheese. Is it red soup or yellow?""

"Uh..." He wracked his brain. "I think he's going to get

whatever looks good." He had lost the conversation somewhere around them staring into each other's eyes.

"Can you call him and remind him that I don't like red soup? Pretty please?"

"I'll text him. I think he said he would get chicken noodle for you." The memory clicked into place, thank goodness. He wasn't that bad of a dad, for which he was grateful.

"Oh, good. Thanks, Daddy."

"You are very welcome, kiddo."

"So we're going to have soup and sammies, and then what?" She looked to him expectantly.

"Well, I thought that we would watch a movie. Sleep." And then? Make out like teenagers. That probably was inappropriate to say to his daughter. But still, he was kind of hoping for at least a few smoochies. He'd thought long and hard about what he wanted, and he was going to jump in with both feet. Or grab the brass ring. Austin would say he was mixing metaphors. It didn't matter.

They didn't have to get to second base. They could just get to home plate without rounding any bases.

"We were thinking about riding tomorrow. Or if you wanted to, we can try snowshoeing. Or we can hang out and make popcorn and have cocoa and play games all day. But I think that Mr. Austin and Dal are going to stay for the weekend."

"Daddy, that is so cool. I can't believe this." She kind of bounced a little bit. "You have to drive faster so that we can get home, so that I can clean up my room. So that Dal can come in and put his stuff— oh, his room is all fixed right? All of his places are fixed places for him to sleep. That aren't scary."

"Right next to your room." He nodded. She'd been very concerned about whether or not Dallas was going to have nightmares. They'd even put in a damn bookshelf.

"You're a good dad. I think I'll keep you. Drive faster."

He shook his head. Nope. Not driving even a single mile faster because that was just stupid. Weather was weather was weather.

"Have you decided about the Christmas tree?" Kyler asked to distract her.

"Uh-huh. We're going to put it up this weekend."

"We are?"

"Yes, with Dal and Mr. Austin there." She stopped for a second and frowned at him. "Daddy? Do we have ormanents?"

They had some, of course, and he'd been bringing them in in dribs and drabs so she didn't notice because he wanted this to be special. They'd discussed it over many, many suppers together at their new kitchen table. Whether or not many colors were better or one color. She'd decided on rainbow colors. Whether there needed to be only balls or all different kinds. She'd voted for all different kinds with balls. Garland Yes. White lights, not multi-colored. But not blinking. He had it all put together.

He'd even found this weird fuzzy white tree skirt that he thought would make her smile. It had a wide red velvet trimming all around it. The only thing he hadn't found was his star. "Well, maybe we should go to the store. Pick up a few things."

"Okay, should we go now? Or should we take Dal and Mr. Austin?"

He tilted his head. "What do you think?"

"I want to go with Dallas," she said. "I know he's not my brother, but I like to have a friend there when we do things. And Mr. Austin really likes you."

"I really like him." And Kyler wanted to like him a lot more. Physically. Like now. "We'll see what they say."

"Cool." She kicked her feet, humming. "Can you—"

"No. I cannot go any faster."

"You are the meanest. Momma would go *so* fast."

"I know she would. And I have asked her many times not to." He and Henley had always disagreed on certain things about safety. "If you won't do it with your horse trailer, don't do it with our kid in the car," he told her all the time.

"I know, Daddy." She sat back with a sigh. "I just get so excited."

"I know, but accidents aren't fun. They're scary as all get out."

"No accidents," she agreed. "I want to be there for Christmas."

"That's right." God, he loved the way she figured things out. "Have you decided if you're going to the ice-skating party with 4-H?"

"No. I mean, no, I haven't decided."

He wondered if Dallas had asked her to do something, or if she worried about ice skating. "Okay. I need to let them know soon so they know how much food they need, kiddo."

"Yeah. I just...I'll decide later."

That was weird. Paige didn't do uncertain.

"What's wrong, honey? Was someone mean to you?" He wanted to dig at this and not let it explode on him later.

"No. I don't have any friends there. I told them that I am not rodeo trashy."

He scowled. "They said you were trashy?"

"Rodeo trashy."

"Well, we're not." And it was on. He was calling the 4-H coordinators as soon as he got home. No one called his kid names.

"I know! I am the daughter of a world-champion barrel racer and a state-champion saddle bronc rider. I got friends everywhere, and my god daddy is a *bullfighter*."

"Yes, ma'am. We are rodeo royalty, dammit." He nodded,

his jaw tight. He hated that people would give Paige a hard time over what he did for a living. In 4-H, for fuck's sake.

"That's right. I am going to be the best racer one day. The best."

"You're already darn good, baby girl. Your momma says so too." She was fearless, and that was half the battle. And his ex knew from good barrel racers.

"So I don't have to go?"

"Not if you don't want to, honey." And that was one less gift he had to buy if she stayed home.

"Okay. Can me and Dallas go ice skating over the break instead?"

"Does he ice skate?"

"He can learn. He's way smarter than his dad thinks."

"Oh, honey, I think his dad thinks he's amazing." He chuckled. "He only worries because Austin is still growing out of a few things that he had when he was really little. Like Tiny Dave, remember him?" Tiny Dave had been the best bull rider on the circuit until he retired just over a year ago.

"Uh-huh, but I know. He can do things. He's not dumb."

"Not a bit. So if Dallas wants to, then y'all can go." They crested the little rise, their itty-bitty ranch came into view. Whew. Sometimes drive-home conversations could be hard.

"That's our house!" Every time they pulled up, she said it, and it made him feel ten feet tall and bulletproof.

"It is. And soon it will have Christmas lights."

"Oh, I love lights." She bounced, then unbuckled her seat belt and slid out of her car seat. "Hey, critters! We're home!"

He shook his head. That had been the longest drive home in history.

"Okay, honey. Come on and let's get cleaned up, and then make sure we have all the sammy stuff. If not, I'll call Mr. Austin and get him to get more cheese."

"Okay, Daddy. Then I'll go make sure Penny and Roany-Bony-Maroney have hay and water."

"Why don't we go together, hmm?" He didn't love the idea of her heading into the barns all on her almost-six-year-old own. "I like hanging out with you."

"Okay! But check the sammy stuff first."

"I will. Go get on your boots." He grinned, watching her run ahead of him. God, she made his heart full.

A text buzzed his phone, and he glanced at it.

<anything else?> Came from AJ.

<just about to check the sandwich sitch>

<no potato. got 2 tomato, 1 chicken noodle, donuts, choc chip cookies>

<Cool> He headed inside, going right to the kitchen. They had plenty of bread, but only sharp cheddar. *<Can you get the white American cheese the kids like?>*

<will do? turkey? ham? frozen pizzas and cheese balls for midnight snack>

<Yes. all of the above> That way they had lunch tomorrow too.

<on it. be there in 1/2 hour>

<See you soon. We might be in the barn> Depended on how much brushing they wanted to do.

<I'll just take the food into the house?>

<Yes. Of course.> Silly man. He was...welcome.

<Cool>

He grinned, because he was thinking how Paige was wanting Dallas to feel like family. He wanted AJ to feel that way too, oddly enough. To feel comfortable. Wanted.

"Okay, Daddy, I'm ready. Let's go love on Penny. She's missed me *all* day."

"Let's hit it, kiddo." He changed out his good coat for his work one, and they were off, heading to the barn. That was one of the joys of his life. Sharing this little ranch with his kid.

Paige sang as she skipped, splashing through the icy mud.

His cowgirl.

She made his heart clench. And more than anything on earth, he wanted her to be happy.

"Penny! Penny, how are you? Roany-boney? Are you in here staying warm?"

He chuckled, because two noses popped right over stall doors. Yeah, they were ready for some company too. He kinda thought neither horse approved of Paige being gone most of the day at school.

She knew this routine as well as she knew her own name, and she went around filling water and pouring sweet feed. She knew to measure, because she'd seen bloat and colic already in her short life, and didn't want that for her buddies.

He checked everyone out, and then they started currycombing, and he listened to her talk about everything from dolls to school to racing to her mom to Dal.

The crunch of gravel under tires sounded sooner than he would have believed, and she kissed Penny's nose. "I got to go get Dal, Penny!"

"Stay away from the car, okay?"

"I will. We'll be right back. She misses Dal too!" And off she went.

"I bet you give no shits, huh, lady?" He put Paige's curry comb away.

Penny blew her lips at him, then bared her teeth.

He got it. He wanted to—

He wanted to make out with AJ. He wanted to kiss a man. He wanted to press their lips together and see how different it was.

He rubbed her nose. "I got some hours yet."

Now that he'd let himself imagine it, let himself admit it, now he was committed. And he was going to get what he wanted.

Tonight.

"Did you see, Poppy? There's a little room that's just for me!"

Austin wasn't sure the bedroom was for Dallas, *specifically*, but he had to admit, it sure screamed specific-little-boy-friendly to him.

The artwork was all Sherlock Holmes and dragons and pirates. There was a chair and table with a puzzle, a bookshelf with a handful of well-loved early chapter books, and a bedside lamp shaped like a dinosaur.

It was stunning, and Austin was touched to the bone.

"I see, bud. That's kind of amazing, huh?"

"You like it, Dal? Daddy let me pick out the puzzle and the dragon pictures!"

"It's so cool! It's like...I have two rooms in two houses!" Dallas hugged Paige hard. "Thank you, so much."

Oh god, that was so sweet.

And even better, it was bedtime, pretty much, and they were getting the kids on the way to a bath each and pajamas and then adult time.

Hallelujah.

He wasn't sure what that meant to Ky, but he was so ready to find out.

It had been six years since he'd been intimate—even made out—with anyone. That seemed nuts now that he thought about it, but it was true.

Nerves were making his stomach feel like it was full of, not butterflies, but bees.

"Come on, you two. Let's get baths and everything."

"Okay, Poppy." Dallas went along with him, Paige to the master with Ky, and soon enough, the kids had been read to and were in bed, leaving him and Ky grinning at each other as they walked into the front room.

"Hey." He was nervous, but not scared. Just nervous.

"Hey." Ky moved close, barely inches separating them. "You ready to go sit for a minute?"

"I am. Sofa?" He wanted to be close enough to touch, even if it didn't go far enough for anything intense.

"You know it." Kyler was vibrating, and there was a new intensity in his blue eyes that made Austin's toes want to curl.

Austin took his hand, and they moved to the sofa, settling side by side. He had to remember that Kyler was new at all this.

Ky chuckled. "Okay. Step one of my clever seduction is ticked off."

"Very nicely done. What's step two?" He turned to face Ky.

"Hmm. Well, I think we're progressing toward making out until we can't see. But how about..." Kyler scooted closer until their knees touched, then turned to face him more completely.

"Oh. We have leg-touching. That's surprisingly hot."

"It is, huh?" Ky sounded breathless, and his cheeks were covered in a sweet blush.

"It is." He grinned, daring to reach out and stroke Kyler's jaw.

"Wow." Ky took a deep breath, then grabbed his hand, tugging him until they were close enough to share breath. "Gonna kiss you now."

Oh, this man got full points for daring. He approved. "I'm in. All the way."

He leaned forward, holding Kyler's gaze.

Those pretty lips opened for him, and he pressed his to them, just holding still for a moment, savoring the heat and softness he found. Then he pressed even closer, tongue flicking Ky's lips.

Kyler's eyes went wide, but he didn't pull away, he didn't tense. Instead, he opened up, tongue touching Austin's, hands on Austin's legs.

"Mmm..." Oh, he did remember how to do this. His heartbeat picked up, and his balls got a little heavier. He wanted to do it again.

And again.

So he did. He tilted his head the other direction, kissing Ky until his vision swam with the need for air. He'd been pushing down his attraction to this man, but their kisses were like a match and gasoline.

Kyler pushed back a bit, as if all of the sudden Ky had decided not to worry, that need superseded nerves. They breathed for a moment, then dove in again, and Kyler reached up with one hand to hold the back of his neck.

He flattened his hand on Ky's belly, drawing slow, lazy circles on those sweet abs. He'd stared at them for hours in his office, and right now Ky was still covered with cloth, but this was better. Far better already.

This was real.

This wasn't Maverick. This was Kyler Hale, his good friend and deep crush, and he was heading into trouble as if he were diving into a pool where he couldn't see the bottom.

And he didn't care.

Ky made a sound deep in his throat, and his free hand slid from Austin's leg up toward his crotch. He opened, letting Kyler know that he was not only welcome, but he was eager as fuck to be touched.

Another hot moan sounded, and Ky pressed that hand to his cock, his zipper pushing against him just enough to make it kinda spicy. Not painful.

"Mmm..." He fought the urge to buck up, his eyelids going heavy.

"Oh, that's the ticket, huh?" Ky said it against his mouth, which made tremors shake him.

"You've got amazing hands." He whispered the words, biting on Kyler's bottom lip.

"I like touching you, AJ." The hand on his neck moved, heading down his back.

He had expected shyness, worry, fear—not this eager confidence.

Yum.

Ky dove back in for another kiss, but those hands never stayed still, and Ky encouraged him to touch as well, twisting into his fingers and humming at the good spots. Sensual man.

He found tight nipples, a sensitive hollow of the throat, ticklish hips. And then he focused on the hard cock straining at Kyler's Wranglers. That was a wondrous thing.

He measured from base to tip, giving Ky a bit of pressure.

"Damn." Kyler tore his mouth free, pressing their foreheads together so he could pant. "That feels amazing, honey."

"You have a great mouth. You make me dizzy as all get-out, if I'm honest."

"I feel the same way." Ky chuckled. "Holler if I get going too fast. I've been doing a lot of fantasizing."

"I'm not worried. I was trying to figure out how to ask if we could cover up or go in your bedroom. I don't want to have to stop and explain this to the kids." He didn't even want to think about the children.

"We can totally go to the bedroom, honey. In fact, I really like that idea." Ky rose, holding out a hand to him.

Well, he'd be damned. He took Ky's hand and stood, drawing them closer together. "Lead the way. I'm so in."

"Come on." Kyler took him to the bedroom, which he'd seen once when he'd needed to take Dal to the bathroom, and Paige had been in the guest bath. It was clean and a little spare, but the bed was huge. A lodgepole pine thing with a cloudlike comforter. Someone liked not being on the road.

"This is lovely." He stroked the comforter, petting it.

"Yeah. I splurged. It's warm." Ky chuckled. "Not that I need it now. I'm on fire, honey."

"No. Maybe later after the sweating." Because there was going to be sweating. "Can I take your shirt off?"

"God, yes." Ky let his arms drop to his sides, waiting for him to unbutton things, he thought.

He understood how to do this part. "Is it weird to say that I'm so ready to learn the real you, not the photoshopped fake you?"

"Yeah? The real me has a few more scars, honey." Ky held his breath when Austin started to pull buttons from holes. He could feel it through his hands.

"I'm glad. The real you is amazing. The cover model is beautiful. Two different things."

"I'm glad you think so." Kyler reached up to touch his cheek.

He leaned into the touch, still unbuttoning the flannel shirt, hunting for skin. When he got it, he slid his hand inside, palm over Ky's pec, Kyler's heart thundering against him.

He was slow, letting one kiss melt into two, into three before he stroked one of the hard nipples.

Kyler shuddered, a low, happy noise escaping him. "Mmmhmm." That vibrated against his mouth.

Oh, that made his toes curl, and he pressed a little more, offering the stiff nipple some friction.

"Uhn." Ky twisted as if to protect that tiny nub, but then turned in to the sensation, letting him give more.

"You smell like heaven." Austin leaned in, nibbling at the cords of Kyler's throat, finding a spot he'd missed while shaving.

"Yeah? I was afraid I smelled like horse." That low chuckle

buzzed against his lips. Ky ran a hand up and down his back, digging in to test his muscles some.

"No. Black pepper and leather and soap." And he was going to remember that for years. He was going to write about it.

"And you smell like Gray Flannel and citrus."

"Is that good?" He hoped so.

"It's perfect." Ky put his face against Austin's neck and breathed deep, which stoked the fire in his belly and made his dick twitch. "You like that. I can feel you, hard against me."

Had anything ever been so hot?

Ever?

"Uh-huh." Austin rocked some. "I like everything you're doing."

His balls were heavy, and he was caught between wanting to push Ky down onto the bed and hump or just letting Kyler drive.

"So do I." Kyler kissed his throat, then his chin, then returned to his mouth for a deeper press of lips on his.

Austin had to touch more, learn the texture of Ky's skin. His hands moved of their own accord, even as Ky feasted from his lips.

This man could so easily become an addiction. He felt so damn right.

"You don't have any tattoos?" It was surprising because most people did. Hell, most people his age did.

Ky snorted. "No. I went with Henley to get matching ones. We were in that ten minutes of in lust and going to get rings."

"Like wedding rings?"

"I guess?" Kyler shrugged. "The guy started with Henley, at any rate, and he laid down one line. She burst into tears, started screaming, and ran out."

"No shit?" He circled one nipple, then traced the line down Ky's ribs. "How long were you all married?"

"We weren't. I don't guess we were ever really thinking about it. I mean, we weren't like faking being together. We were together, and we're still good friends, but neither one of us wanted each other forever."

Well, Austin supposed that was a good idea then, that they didn't get their rings tattooed.

"What about you? Any ink?"

Austin shook his head. "No, I thought about it. In fact, I thought about getting ink for every book. And then I realized when I wrote about tattoos and books, they got about halfway through the book, and I discovered I'd never talked about them again. I figure if they're that easy to forget as a writer, they'll be that easy to forget on me."

Ky gave him a wicked, wolfish not-smile. "If I watched you get a tattoo I'd remember every second."

That amazing heaviness in the air between them reappeared. For a second there, Austin couldn't breathe. He wanted Kyler more than anyone he could think of.

So he dove back into kisses, his hands on Ky's back, tugging him close enough no air could get between them.

He groaned, tugging his sweater up so they could be belly to belly. Lord, that was fine.

Ky traced his skin, drawing patterns on his bare lower back. "God, you're fine."

"I want to touch you." He wanted to make Ky come, over and over again.

"Anything you want, honey. I mean it."

He reached down, cupped Ky's ass and drew them tighter together so they could rub.

"Mmm." That growl was so hot, and Kyler rocked against him, cock hard as stone, those hands never still.

Now all he had to do was find a way to get their jeans open.

"What?" Ky pulled back to watch him when he struggled a little.

"Jeans. They need to go."

"Oh." Ky stared down at them. "God yes."

"Jeans and then bed? I don't want to fall down in pure need." Oh, that was classy.

"Naked all the way and bed," Ky countered. "Socks are so porny."

"Yes. So porny, but at least you have your boots off already." He started working Kyler's belt open.

"I do." Ky helped him, yanking it free of the loops to drop it on the floor, the buckle landing with a *thud*.

He did love a confident man. He worked open Ky's fly, letting his fingers brush the hard cock. And it was desperately hard. Long. Hot as a brand.

Perfect.

"Gonna make my knees weak." Ky sounded like he meant it.

"Bed now, then." He skimmed Kyler's jeans and boxer briefs down and off, then helped with the pornalicious socks. Then he knelt at the edge of the bed, dragging his hands up along the muscled thighs.

"Oh God." Ky dug one hand into his hair. "Somehow you still have clothes on."

"Uh-huh. It's a shame." He pushed closer, running his nose along the crease where leg met torso.

"You—Fuck. Austin." Every muscle in Ky's lower body tensed.

"You smell like heaven." He let his cheek rasp along Ky's cock.

"You— God. That's crazy, how good that feels."

Right. Kyler hadn't ever felt a five o'clock shadow, from what he'd said.

He rubbed again, teasing with a long, slow caress.

"Mmpph." The sound burst out of Ky, and his hips jerked like a mad thing, a drop of pre-come appearing at the tip of his cock.

He went to lick it off, then he met Ky's gaze. "Can I?"

"God, yes. Please." Ky nodded, his gaze bright and feverish.

Austin was fixin' to show Kyler what it was like to have a man who adored to suck cock loving on him. He nuzzled, breathing deep one last time, then licked the tip, tongue pressing the slit, before he closed his lips around the head.

A hard grunt was his reward, Ky dancing for him, swaying back and forth.

He closed his eyes and focused, trying to find all the hot spots, tracing the thick veins on the shaft. He loved the softness of the skin over the amazing hardness, and Ky wasn't small, to say the least.

The thoughts of the things they could do together made his body clench, made his prick throb against his zipper.

He wrapped his lips around Ky's cockhead, moaning deep and low as salt and bitter flavors hit his tongue. Kyler pushed in, then pulled back, thrusting in a shallow way, but it wasn't enough. Austin grabbed that muscled ass and tugged.

"Oh fuck!" Ky cried out, hands opening and closing on his shoulders.

Oh, that was hot as anything, that wild need.

"Austin. I'm close, honey." Ky rubbed his shoulder with one hand, the other going back to his hair.

He could tell, and he wasn't scared. In fact, he wanted this to be the best orgasm in the history of the world. He focused on doing what he'd want someone to do for him.

He took Ky down to the root, swallowing convulsively around the tip, demanding Kyler's orgasm.

He wanted Ky to blow his top.

"Austin…" Ky gave him what he wanted, hot seed that spilled into him, making him hum and keep moving, working until Ky tugged at his hair.

He patted the fading cock, then sat on the bed, still fully clothed. "Good?"

"Addled." Kyler blinked at him. "You're all dressed."

"I know. Weird." He tore his sweater off, then started on his jeans.

Ky helped, hands clumsy at first, but then gaining his usual cowboy dexterity. This was a man who knew how to shape leather into intricate shapes. He could open clothes.

Once he was naked, Ky eased him down onto the mattress, pushing close as if he was scared to leave space between them.

"You're making me dizzy." He needed a touch, more kisses, something, but he didn't want to push too far, demand too much.

"Good. You— I never felt anything…damn, AJ."

"That's what I wanted. I wanted to make you feel like heaven." He had needed for Ky to think he was something special.

"It worked." Kyler chuckled against his collarbone, licking a blisteringly hot line along his skin. Those hands slipped down his belly, teasing him, petting him on the way to his cock.

He arched up, his body rocking, his abs pulling in tight. Austin moaned, his whole self waiting for that touch to his dick.

"Oh, you like that, huh?"

"Does a bear shit in the woods?"

"I think so." Ky chuckled. "I mean, where else?" Ky took him in a firm grip and stroked nice and hard.

Oh, what was the question?

His eyes crossed and he spread, leaning into that sure, perfect touch. Austin was pretty sure Ky was damn good at whatever he put his mind to, and he was loving on Austin with a single-minded intensity.

He couldn't breathe, it was so good.

"Kiss me again, AJ."

"Over and over and over again." He pushed up into their kiss, his eyes rolling back into his head.

Kyler moaned against his mouth, hand moving faster on him, that lean, hard body so strong against his. It felt like the best kind of dream, but it was very real.

It had been so long, and he wanted this so bad, that he wasn't going to hold out long.

Not at all.

"Come on, honey. I want to see you come. Next time you can have my mouth, but this time I want to watch your face."

He let out a long, low moan, his entire body shivering as his balls drew up.

"That's it. I can feel you. You're so close." The base of Ky's hand bumped his balls, which had drawn up tight.

"Uhn. Uh-huh." He humped up, and his eyes slammed shut as he shot, his teeth rattling as seed coated Ky's hand.

"Damn." Ky's voice shook. "Damn, honey. You're so fucking *fine.*"

Oh, that felt so good to hear. He loved that. "Thank you."

"Mmmhmm." Kyler kissed him, gently this time, both of them a little silly and sated.

"Can...Do you want me to go..." He wanted to sleep in here. He loved snuggling.

"No. I want you to stay with me." Ky grinned. "Though we might have to put some shorts back on. The kids... we need to leave the door unlocked."

"Yes to both. Dads first, lovers second." That was not even in question.

"Yeah." Ky got up and made his way to the bathroom, coming back with a warm, wet cloth to clean them both up.

It was the tiniest bit awkward, but it wasn't the worst thing ever. He'd been in way worse situations after orgasm.

They pulled on their shorts and cuddled in the bed together, which made the weirdness fade in seconds. Ky felt warm and good and right in his arms.

"This feels...amazing," he admitted.

"It does. I fantasized about this." Ky chuckled, the air brushing his chin. "The orgasms and the sleeping together."

"Yeah. I'm glad you're...here with me." Austin kissed his cheek.

"Me too." Kyler hugged him close, then laughed. "Want me to turn on that movie?" They had both fallen asleep on the couch more than a few times watching a movie together.

"Sounds great. It's obviously our favorite sleeping aid."

"I think that might be changing though." Ky's fingers splayed across the small of his back, and yeah. He could get that.

"Mmhmm..." His eyes crossed, and he snuggled in. "Thank you. I needed this."

"So did I, honey. So did I." Ky just stayed right there, holding on, and he could sleep like this for sure.

In fact, he worried that he might want to stay like this all the time.

Chapter Fifteen

Kyler woke up to the sound of giggling.

He was warm, his body snuggled up to something firm and wonderful, and he didn't want to move. But that giggling was out in the front room, and that was... ominous.

He opened his eyes, finding his arms full of tall, gangly, pale man.

He couldn't stay here.

He had to figure out what the kids were doing.

Had to.

"Hey." He shook AJ real gentle, amazed at how easy it was to wake up with him. "The kids are up to something."

"Oh fuck. Okay." AJ woke up, lurching up to standing. "I'm up, I'm up."

"Mmmmhmm." He rolled out of bed. "Clothes." They had both pulled on their shorts, but they really needed sweats at least. He grabbed a pair and shrugged on a T-shirt.

AJ threw on his jeans and sweater from last night, hopping into socks. "Fuck, it's cold. Hopefully they're not cooking."

"God forbid." He shuddered. "Or on the ladder trying to put up more decorations."

"Shut your mouth." AJ shot him a horrified glance. "Can you imagine?"

"No. Yes. God." He skimmed into his socks, then sprinted for the front room, his morning wood totally deflated. "Paige?"

"Yes, Daddy?" Paige smiled up at him, a box of Corn Flakes and a huge bowl in front of the kids, two spoons stuck in. "We're watching *Paw Patrol*!"

Relief made him sag for a moment. "Oh, cool. How much milk did you leave?" He'd been planning on pancakes, but it seemed like cereal was the breakfast of the day.

"We wanted yogurt in it, and you promised pancakes."

Dallas nodded, smiled. "This is a snack. A par-feet. I read about it."

"Parfait," AJ corrected, heading for the coffee machine.

Kyler chuckled. "Yogurt, huh?" He grabbed the cereal box to close it up. Nothing was worse than stale cereal. "Well, thank you for being so careful."

"We don't want Santa to get mad, Daddy!" Paige's eyes went wide. "Santa watches. All. The. Time."

Santa as serial killer stalker. Yay.

Dallas nodded, so serious. "He sees you when you're asleep."

"He knows when you do bad thi-i-ings," AJ sang, sotto voce.

His lips twitched. They were in such trouble.

"We didn't, Poppy! I promise. We didn't make a mess. We watched our shows. We are so good."

AJ chuckled. "I believe you."

"Did you and Daddy watch movies in Daddy's room?" Paige asked.

He glanced at AJ, but it was his kid who'd asked, so he

guessed it was on him. "We did. You know our couch isn't as broken in as Mr. Austin's."

"I know, and it's not big like his either. It's good, because your bed is big, and so are you and Mr. Austin."

"Poppy is so tall," Dallas put in.

"He is at that." He sent Austin a long glance.

"True story." AJ handed him his cup of coffee, then went back to make his own.

"Thanks." He sipped, humming at the hot, strong brew. He'd need it to make pancakes and wrangle some very excited kids.

"Anytime. Do you hooligans want hot chocolate?"

"Does your daddy have marshmallows?" Dallas whispered.

"Uh-huh," Paige said in the loudest stage whisper ever. "Big ones, little ones, and ones with chocolate inside."

"Chocolate in marshmallow *in* chocolate?" Dallas grabbed his chest and toppled backward.

"I know!"

Kyler rolled his eyes, his grin too big to contain. God, he did love those two.

"So, I assume that's a yes?"

"Poppy! Didn't you hear?"

Austin's eyes went comically wide. "I heard!"

"You want some hot chocolate in your coffee, honey?" He paused, wondering if it was okay to call AJ honey in front of the kids.

"Oh, that sounds good. How about you? I can make three cups, and we'll share the last one."

"That sounds grand." He liked sharing.

"Perfect." AJ moved around his kitchen as though he belonged there, and Kyler loved it. He wanted to see more.

They'd spent a lot of time at Austin's condo while their house was getting finished, he loved how AJ looked in his house. How easy it was for the kids to settle in.

They fit better here. Dallas and AJ made the house seem less…big.

"Daddy! Are we gonna finish stringing all the lights and put up the stuff?"

"We are, kiddo."

"Can I help? I want to be part of your family too. Poppy says you and Paige are part of ours!"

Paige smiled up at him, nodding as if to say 'don't fuck this up, Daddy'.

"I had planned on it, Dal." He ruffled Dallas's hair. "That's why you guys spent the night." Among other reasons.

"Oh, good. Good. I love helping. No one here hates me."

"No one hates you, son," Austin said, and Paige rolled her eyes.

"Yeah, they so do."

He glanced at AJ again, and Austin shook his head slightly, so he let it go. AJ could talk to Dal. "Well, we adore you."

"I'm glad. I like being your family. Paige is my best friend in the whole world. When she grows up, I'm going to be her maiden honor at her wedding."

"Wow. That's pretty cool." He grinned, thinking of adult Dallas in a bubblegum-pink dress with a bow on the butt.

AJ chuckled softly. "Where do you keep the magical marshmallows, man?"

"In the cabinet next to the fridge on the top shelf." Where Paige couldn't reach, even with her stepstool. She could devour a whole bag in one sitting.

"Ah, I understand. That never works with me, you know."

No. No, Austin had a great length of leg.

"I can see that." He grinned as AJ grabbed the bag of marshmallows and tried one, his eyebrows rising. "Yum. Best go sparing on those, though, huh?"

"Oh, they'll run it off."

"Can we each have half, Poppy Austin?" Paige asked. "Otherwise it fills the whole cup and it's gloopy."

"Yes, ma'am." That was his girl. He had dried mini marshmallows for when they wanted more halfway through. He fixed up cups, handing them out, then grabbed a bowl to stir pancakes. "Can you start that electric griddle, Austin?"

"Sure. No problem." AJ smiled at him, and he felt it, deep in his balls.

He felt like a teenager, like he could start bouncing at any moment.

The kids were moaning over the marshmallows, and he whipped the batter, then started the sausages. It was... He loved the vibe of how they were together.

How come it had never been like this with Henley?

As soon as he had the thought, he knew it wasn't fair. Henley and he had been younger, they'd been rodeoing, they'd been nomadic, and their energy had a totally different vibe.

Henley and he had been kerosene and lightning. AJ was warm, but not fiery, like snuggling together under the perfect blanket on a winter's day, a fire crackling in the fireplace and snow falling outside.

He was easy enough that Kyler knew he would have to work hard not to take it all for granted.

It would be so easy. AJ seemed as if he'd always been here, somehow.

It was magical and a little scary, all at once.

"You okay?"

"Huh?" Kyler glanced down and realized he was standing there with his whisk in his bowl, not moving. "Just admiring."

"What? I— Oh!" AJ blinked at him, eyes going wide. "Me?"

"Yes." He winked, which made Austin flush. That was adorable.

How anyone had walked away from this man, from Dallas was beyond him.

From *baby* Dallas.

"Daddy! What are you going to put in the pancakes?"

"Do you want blueberries or pecans?" He cut her right off from asking for more chocolate. That, she didn't need.

"Dal? Booberries or nutties?"

"Booberries!" Dallas was so excited. "I love booberries."

"Paige?" he asked.

"Yep!"

"Okay, you got it." That had gone easily. He was always grateful when that shit happened. Paige was a lot like a really rank horse sometimes—smart and wicked and not particularly easy to please.

The pancakes came up piping hot, blueberries bursting out, and he warmed the syrup while Austin put the sausage on a paper towel-lined plate to drain off the grease.

"Breakfast, ahoy!" he called.

"It is time to have breakfast," Paige said, shaking her butt all the way over to the kitchen table, her crookedy pigtails bouncing like weird springs. Dallas, on the other hand, followed more quietly with less bouncing. On his hands.

"You know that kid is really good at gymnastics," Kyler noted.

"I know." AJ grinned at him, shook his head like he was a touch bemused. "Go figure, right? He's got too much length of leg though. He's gonna be tall. I think, at least."

"You gonna let him be on the team?"

AJ shrugged. "There's time to think about that, I guess. I'm not opposed to it necessarily, although those little girls that are on the team here, they're fierce, they're very committed. Those dads spend a lot of time on the weekends at events."

"Rodeo dads are the same. We spend a lot of time driving

back and forth. Unloading and reloading horse trailers. And then there's fair season..."

"Fair season. They have rodeos at fairs?"

God, Austin was cute.

"Well, sure. But I meant show animals for that, you know? Chickens, rabbits, goats, calves, that sort of thing."

AJ tilted his head. "Who do you show them to?"

"Judges. You get ribbons and stuff."

"Oh." AJ took one of the kids' plates to the table and got Dallas settled. "Well that's cool. I'm a big fan of ribbons. So you and Paige would take Jennifer the chicken to the fair to show her."

Paige nodded. "And then you sell it."

Dallas blinked her. "You'd sell Jennifer?"

Paige frowned. "Who's Jennifer?"

"The chicken."

"What chicken?"

Austin grabbed the milk. "The chicken you're going to sell at the fair."

"Wait." Dallas glared at Paige. "You can't sell Jennifer. What if she's friendly? What if she lays the golden egg? You're going to sell Jennifer the golden egg chicken!"

Somehow, Kyler had lost control of the entire situation. He wasn't sure how, but he knew it was happening.

"No one is going to sell Jennifer," Kyler said, buttering Paige's pancakes for her.

"Daddy, we don't have chickens yet. Are we going to name one Jennifer?"

He stifled a grin. He would be willing to bet they did when they got chickens in the spring. "I think this is what you call a hypothetical situation, kiddo. Do you remember what that is?"

"Like a daydream that may or may not come true?"

"Something like that, yeah."

"Nice." AJ's approval felt surprisingly good. It wasn't that Kyler thought that his kid was stupid. No way. He knew better. But sometimes Dallas was so smart, it was just a little intimidating. So to see Paige make those connections, and to feel like Austin understood what she had going on with her? That felt damn fine.

"Can we have a chicken, Poppy?" Dallas asked around a mouthful of pancakes.

"Son, we're hiding the cat. I think chickens are probably out of the question. I am relatively sure you can't teach her chicken to poop in the litter box." AJ winked when Kyler snort-chuckled.

Kyler didn't bother to mention that it was a bit unreasonable to ask a cat and the chicken to share an apartment. There were worse pairings, he was sure, but that one was yeah, no.

"You could have a bunny," Paige said. "Bunnies stay in cages."

"We really don't have room for a bunny, Paige," AJ said. "I'm sorry."

"How about a llama? You could put him in the car park."

Austin poured syrup over his pancakes, then began to eat. "I don't know that I've ever even met a llama in person."

That made Kyler blink and tilt his head. "Really? You've never seen a llama?"

I'm pretty sure. Maybe. You would think I'd remember that. They're awfully cute, with their big eyelashes and the funny hats."

"I think they only wear the funny hats in Peru."

"What's Peru, Poppy?" Dallas asked.

"It's a country in South America, with a bunch of mountains, and llamas, and Machu Picchu."

Paige's eyes went wide. "What is a pachu pichu?"

"Machu." Austin repeated, drawing the word out.

Paige grinned and she and Dallas said together, "Machu."

"Picchu." AJ was obviously having too much fun.

"Pickachu!" Paige said.

"Pew pew!" Dallas added, shooting the air with a finger gun.

"You guys are nutbags," Kyler told them, and they dissolved into giggles. "We'll have to show you Machu Picchu after breakfast."

"After we go outside and play, Daddy?" Paige asked. "There's snow."

"And after we finish decorating," Dallas agreed.

"We have a full day." AJ polished off his sausage. "I like it."

"Me too." Kyler liked this whole situation a lot. He gave Austin one of his best smiles, because that thought was for him alone.

"Well, finish eating, hooligans. That snow is waiting for y'all to make snow angels." AJ licked his fork clean of syrup.

"Okay, Poppy." Dallas beamed, and Paige giggled, stuffing her mouth full, and Kyler felt like the luckiest damn man on earth.

He would play this one by ear and enjoy it for now. See where it went.

Lord knew he was the king of that.

Chapter Sixteen

"Where's Dallas?"

"Northeast Texas." He had to tease. Austin loved seeing Stoney and Ford. He'd met them at their dude ranch. Back before he had broken up with the evil ex. Back then his life had been full of things like gay ski week or gay brunches. The gay lifestyle. Now he was just a single dad.

"Don't make me kill you, man," Stoney chuckled. "I got shit to do."

Stoney plopped down on the sofa at the coffee shop, waving his hand at Ford, so dramatic. "Go on now, get me a latte."

Austin stared at the cowboy. Obviously, something was going on. Possibly somebody had lost a bet. Because he knew Stoney, and Stoney had never waved his hand, limp-wristedly in the entirety of his time on earth. Nor was Ford the kind of man who accepted the, you know, 'go fetch my slippers, boy' kind of situation.

Ford and Stoney took a beat, then they both cracked up, and Ford cuffed Austin's shoulder. "You need anything?"

Austin shook his head. "No, no. Thanks, though. I've got a caramel white chocolate something coming. It's up there on the specials board. It looks amazing. It's got nutmeg. I figure, you know, it's Christmas. Nutmeg."

"Okay, so I'll be right back." Ford headed off to the counter.

Austin stared at Stoney askance. "What the hell is going on?"

Stoney snorted. "Nothing. We were talking about this couple that we met. They came to stay at the ranch. They were hilarious, but obviously one was the Lord of the Manor and the other one was all fetch and carry. I didn't ask; I don't want to know. But we were talking about it on the way here, and I got tickled. I thought maybe I'd try it."

Austin shook his head. "Yeah, I don't think that's gonna work for you."

"Probably not. So come on, where's Dallas? I wanted to see his little face."

Someone was missing his son. Quartz was away at his first year of college and was due home, he was sure, for Christmas, but Stoney was definitely feeling empty-nest syndrome.

"He's with his best friend Paige and her daddy. They're doing something that involves outdoor sports. And horses. And since I only rarely do outdoor sports, and I don't do horses, they're doing it without me."

"Horses, huh? That's cool. Mr. Dallas gonna grow up to be a cowboy like me?"

"I sincerely doubt it, but it's a possibility. Who knows?" He shrugged, grinned. "I'm dating one."

He thought.

They weren't really dating; they were more like having a life and sleeping together, which was an awful lot like being married, except that he went home to his condo five nights a week. Three nights a week. Some days a week?

"Oh my God, you're dating a cowboy? What the hell?" Stoney made big, wide eyes, the expression patently fake.

"I know. It's Dallas's fault."

"So where did you meet him?"

Oh, that was a complicated story. He wasn't sure he was going to tell it either. Because there was meeting, and then there was *meeting*. They'd sort of met on a super meta level almost a year ago.

Of course, Stoney River was not the most meta human being alive, so maybe he'd just stick with the facts, ma'am. "Our children are best friends. They met at school. Kyler has this amazing little girl—fierce as hell. She will kick somebody's butt if they need it. The absolute polar opposite of Dallas in every way, and Dallas would, I think, go to war for her."

"Dude. That's too cool. So then, you what, meet said girl dad at a play date, and you fall for him? Splat?"

He snorted. "I met him at the school office when his daughter punched a kid in the face for bullying Dallas."

"Oh, man. Shit's gotten Western up in your life."

"What?" Ford strolled back over to put chocolate croissants on the table. "You cowboying up, Austin?"

"He's dating one, honey. His kid's best friend's dad."

"Holy shit. No way." Ford grinned, eyes sparkling. "Look at you. Once you go cowboy..."

"Oh, shut up." He winked at Ford. "I can't even. It was just serendipity."

Stoney chuckled. "So tell us about him, man. What do you know about him?"

"He was a rodeo man. A bronc rider. And Paige's mom is a barrel racer."

"Oh yeah. What's her name?" Stoney asked. He followed the rodeo.

Austin shrugged. "It's Henley something. I'm sure that Kyler has told me her last name, I just don't remember."

Stoney's eyes lit up. "Henley Morgan? She's good. National champion. She's got a little girl, too. Uh..." Stoney rubbed his forehead and his temple. "Hale. Does that sound right?"

"That's him. Kyler Hale."

Stoney snorted. "I thought he was straight."

"Bisexuality is a thing, my friend."

"Hey, I know. I judge not. I think it's cool. Have you met his wife?"

Ford kicked Stoney's boot. "Ex-wife."

"Neither. Never married. But have I met Paige's mom? No, not yet. She's coming for Christmas." And hadn't that been a nightmare? He was supposed to be going home to see his folks, and Dallas had lost his shit, insisting that this was Paige's Christmas with her daddy, and if they missed this Christmas then they were going to miss next Christmas. And that would mean three whole Santa Clauses before he could see Paige at Christmas.

Austin would probably have fought harder if what Dallas wanted wasn't exactly what he desired too. So he'd given in. If they were going to be a thing, him and Ky, Dallas was going to have to get used to splitting time. And sharing his step-sister with someone.

And thank God no one could hear what he was thinking because they'd been sleeping together for like ten days. It was a little early to be all step-sister, step-brother, rings and forever and...

But it was what he wanted. He couldn't help it. Austin believed. He believed in the whole falling in love and happily ever after shit. It wasn't something he put on a page because he got paid to do it. He fucking believed.

Now he had to manage getting through however long it took before Ky believed it, too.

"That ought to be interesting," Stoney said with an evil grin.

Ford thumped him. "Blended families exist. As you well know."

"We're not there, but Dallas and Paige are thick as thieves."

"So you're meeting Henley for Christmas? Y'all ought to come up for the big Christmas party on the twenty-second. Kids are welcome..." Stoney winked at him. "So are blended families."

"Lord have mercy. I'll ask. I bet Ky would like to meet everyone. He's a little like an island."

"Having you say that is something, man," Ford teased.

"I know!" He chuckled. "He's a lot like me, oddly. Not so much bookish, though I've seen his reading stash now. Murder mysteries and westerns. But he works from home making saddles and stuff, and he takes Paige all over the damn Roaring Fork to activities, and I think most of his old friends kind of abandoned him when Paige came along..."

"Well, is Henley involved in Paige?" Stoney asked, and he nodded.

"She really is. She travels a lot, of course, but she's on her way back from the NFR and a little vacation. She's staying with Kyler until the stock show in Denver. Then she's off again."

"Neat." Ford chuckled. "I'm kind of stunned. I mean, you were always so... I dunno. Gay agenda."

"I haven't gotten any less gay, man. He's the bi one, not me."

"Are you worried about having his ex stay with him?"

He shrugged. "Why? If he'd wanted her, he could have stayed with her. Hell, you should see the moms at the gym, at the trampoline park, at all the places."

Can you have coffee, Kyler?

Oh, Kyler, can you come over and polish my light bulbs?

Kyler, would you be a dear and pick up this big, heavy bag for me?

If Kyler wanted a lady-friend to sleep with, he had plenty of opportunity.

"Besides," he said, warming to his topic. "It's amazing that she's so involved with Paige. She's not phoning it in. She loves that little girl, and she and Ky are still good friends."

"That's awesome, man. I mean, it really helps if everyone is on good terms."

"Sure." Not that Ford and Stoney had to worry about that. Stoney's baby momma had, sadly, passed. But it was a complicated family thing for them, nonetheless.

"Do you have any new books out? You could do another signing at the ranch for Ski Week. That was a huge success last year."

Oh, he didn't know. He was sort of slacking, but...

"I can do that. I'm going to start a new series."

Ford winked. "Something with a rancher?"

"Shut up."

Stoney hooted. They called Ford for the coffees, and he went to grab them, coming back licking his lips. "You're right, man. That's a good latte."

"They're Quartz's favorite."

"How is he? Coming home soon?"

Stoney lit up. "He is! And I'm not ashamed to admit that I'm ready. I wasn't prepared for how weird it would be for him to be gone. He's finishing his last final today, packing up his stuff tomorrow to put into storage, and then flying home the day after. I'm so ready."

"And the ranch baby?"

"Having her third birthday."

"That's too cool." Stoney and Ford had a bunch of kids living at their ranch thanks to their hands, but their ranch chef, Geoff, and his partner had a grandbaby who was the light of everyone's lives. Such a sweetie.

"Yeah. We need more babies around, you know?"

"We'll get puppies," Ford murmured.

Stoney just gave him a blink, and Ford blew him a kiss.

"God help me, with Dal spending so much time at Kyler's property, he wants a dog. A chicken named Jennifer. Llamas. We did a whole reading afternoon about Machu Picchu."

"Machu Picchu? Seriously?" Stoney grinned. "You do have a fascinating little boy."

"I detect no lies." Yeah, Dallas was the neatest boy in the whole wide world. "Paige is pretty cool too. I've never met anyone—no man, woman, or beast—who was more fearless. And competitive? She wasn't reading at all, and then she found out that Dallas was reading chapter books, and suddenly she's a reader."

"And these two are in kindergarten?"

"Yep. The teacher is absolutely stunned. I'm fairly sure Dallas was born knowing how to read, but Paige doesn't intend to be left behind on anything." Austin kind of worried about that, to be honest. Maybe on the gymnastic things Dallas would excel, but Paige was so much better than he was at damn near everything else. Riding, sports, even just normal, everyday niceties of life, like being able to be a functional kid.

They were good for each other. They pushed each other to be better.

"I'm glad that you like her, man. It's always hard if you don't like your significant other's kid." Ford winked over at Stoney, who rolled his eyes.

"Good thing you like mine," Stoney shot back.

His significant other... God. It seemed too soon to say that, but his whole self screamed, "Yes!" when Ford said it.

"Good thing." Nothing phased Ford. Not really.

"Make sure you ask if everyone wants to come to the party.

It's not fancy, just good food. Carols. There will be presents for the kiddos. It's not a formal thing."

Because God knew Stoney was all about formal.

"I will. I can't think of a good reason that they'd say no."

"Well, if they do, you'll come up, the two of you. We'd love to see you."

He nodded, but they all knew he wouldn't go by himself. That was a lot of driving in the snow, in the dark. Ky had been on the road so much and so often that no kind of driving bothered him, so if he would go, then Austin trusted him to get them all there.

"Okay, Stoney. We need to get going," Ford said, rising. He gave Austin a one-armed hug. "Good to see you, man. Seriously."

"It was good to be seen. Y'all have a good time Christmas shopping, and I can't wait to see Quartz and hear about his first semester at USC."

Stoney nodded. "You wrote an amazing reference letter for him. I'll never be able to pay you back for that."

"I doubt that the reference letter from the romance writer carried near as much weight as the one from his math and his science teacher, but you're welcome."

The guys wandered off, and he settled in with his coffee playing on his phone, taking notes, people watching.

Normal stuff.

He loved to sit at the coffee shop and listen to gossip, listen to the interactions between people.

Imagine a little bit what different folks were doing at different times.

Like that one couple who were sitting over there.

One of them was mad, red-faced, and the other one was talking hard, like to beat the band.

Was it unfair?

Maybe so. Maybe they'd lost their job, and they were

trying to explain how they were going to make it work over Christmas. Maybe the one guy wanted to go home for Christmas and the other guy wanted to stay in town.

Oh.

Or what if there was a secret baby?

It could happen. This one guy had a baby.

Three years ago or so, maybe he'd been a sperm donor. And all of a sudden, the mom had died and now there was going to be a baby.

And this other guy was like, 'I don't want to have any kids. I don't really like kids.'

And other guy was going, Mr. Redhead was going, 'But this is my kid. Don't you love my kid?'

And Mr. Dark Hair was saying, 'How do you even know it's yours? What were you doing jacking off in a cup for anyway?'

And the redhead—what was a good name for a redhead? Scotty, that could be Scotty—Scotty was saying, 'Well, don't you remember we had that bill, Jim? When the pipes broke on the new house and had to be fixed and we didn't know where it was going to come from? I didn't want you to have to put extra shifts in at the... Police station? No fire station. Fire station?'

That was it.

And that was when Mr. Dark-Haired Jim had to admit that he did remember and that it was kind of sweet that someone would jack off into a cup for broken pipes.

But on the other hand, there was this baby.

And what if there were more babies?

What if they ended up with ten thousand babies? That all looked like, umm, Scotty. Scotty the redhead, Scotty the Scot O'Houlihan. What if there were ten thousand Scotty the Scot O'Houlihan babies running around the Roaring Fork corridor?

That was actually a pretty good idea.

Not the ten thousand babies part, but the whole idea; that was pretty good.

There could be a book.

That would be a sweet book to come out in the summertime, a summer beach read.

With a fireman and Scotty Scot O'Houlihan, the... Scot-Irish...barista.

That was it.

A barista.

The Fireman and the Barista: A Colorado story.

Oh, he even had a title.

He was going to have to put in his schedule with his editor, and say, "if I get this book to you by Valentine's Day, we could have it out in time for Beach Reads."

He'd get hold of Alex, his cover artist, say he wanted something soft and gentle and charming with a baby.

There had to be a baby on the front, a redheaded baby and a big strong man cradling him.

Her.

It didn't matter, it was a baby. Babies could be gender-neutral. With boots.

Not the baby, the man.

The man needed boots.

He took a whole bunch of notes, and then shot off a note to his editor so that she didn't have a heart attack when an extra book came and plopped into her inbox.

His phone buzzed, and he glanced at it, expecting his editor.

It was Ky.

<*We're all missing you, and everyone is cold. How about the holiday market for a bit? Meet us there?*>

Oh, poor kiddos. <*I'd love that. I'll head over now.*>

<*Cool. We'll see you there. You got coffee?*>

<Yep>

<K. I'll get hot cocoas>

<Want a coffee for u?> Because he was thinking about getting one of those cinnamon toast things...

<Please> He got a little crazy smiley, the crossed eyes making him laugh.

Austin went up and ordered two cinnamon toast lattes to go, humming "O Come All Ye Faithful" under his breath.

They'd missed him.

God, that felt so good.

Chapter Seventeen

"Hey, what's going on?" Kyler navigated a snowbank at the crosswalk, the plows having done a number on them during the night. He felt as if he were climbing Denali to get to the coffee shop, his hands full of last-minute shopping bags, and Henley on the damn phone. Finally. She'd been out of touch for three days, ever since she'd called to tell him she would be late.

"Shit, Ky, what hasn't been going on." She sounded exhausted; he knew her well enough to know her tells there. "About the time I was ready to leave, Blaze got into something in the boarding stable and came down with a case of colic. Not bad enough to really hurt her, but I had to walk her every hour for ten minutes for a day, then find another place for them to stay."

"You could bring them with you, Henley." He almost ran into a guy who came charging out of a jewelry shop, face like a thundercloud.

"I am, but I needed Blaze to be road-ready first." She sighed. "And then Momma fell and broke her wrist."

"Jesus. Well, that explains why you didn't come straight from Vegas. Is she going to be okay?"

"Yeah. Yeah, Bentley is with her now, but it was a big mess. I'm sorry. I mean, I meant to be there days ago. But I'm half a day out now, and I'll be there tonight."

"Okay, cool." Not that he would tell Paige until Henley was there. Paige was pretty peeved at her mom. "Did you bring something nice to wear? We got a big party to go to tomorrow night."

"What kind of party? Like, do I have to wear a dress, because I'm not wearing a dress."

"It's at a ranch. I can't see that a dress would be necessary." AJ had said that a couple of his friends owned a dude ranch outside of town a ways, and they were having a kid-friendly party. But he'd also said that it could get a little fancy up in there, so Kyler was going to have to wear his good jacket. He wasn't sure yet what Paige was going to wear.

"Oh, I totally have something sparkly for a Christmas party. No worries. I got Paige a bunch of presents, by the way. Clothes and some toys and all. She says she's excited to introduce me to her friend."

"Yeah, about that..." He was going to have to tell her that he and AJ were sleeping together. He imagined Austin would be fine sleeping on the couch when he spent the night or just not spending the night at all.

But that was a long time. She was going to be at the house for two weeks.

"Are they fighting? Paige didn't say so when I talked to her this morning. She was with him, in fact, and his dad."

"She is. They're at some kind of party for the gymnastics place. I drew the long straw so I could finish up my shopping."

She laughed, that throaty sound so familiar. "So domestic."

"Screw you, Hen. Anyway, I should warn you, uh—" He

glanced around, trying to find the damn coffee shop. Another half a block. "I'm dating Paige's friend's dad."

There. Woo. He'd said it.

"No shit. I was wondering if you were ever gonna come out of the closet."

"There really wasn't a closet to come out of."

"Oh, honey, I'm not accusing you of anything. I saw how you looked at the cowboys. And the cowgirls. I always figured one day we'd have a threesome. Your new guy bi?"

"I don't think so." He couldn't help his laugh there. AJ seemed to be the absolute queerest person he knew. Possibly was the queerest man alive.

Although that probably wasn't fair. They had a whole gay ski week here in Aspen. In a couple of months, he would totally be excited to see what that was like.

"That's a shame. I also am not bi. I like dick. But then again, so do you."

"Henley..."

"Wasn't it you started it? I'm not the one sleeping with my daughter's best friend's father."

He nodded. And tried to figure out what the hell he was going to get AJ for Christmas. "Oh, even better. I'm the cover model for his romance novels."

There was a long pause. "You have *got* to be shitting me."

"No. You know, I had to pay for some things at the house —" And he explained the whole sordid story, which was not particularly sordid, but all he could do was kind of shrug and blush and stammer.

"I think that's adorable. I mean, seriously. You're a Fabio. Does Paige know?"

She had never mentioned it, so he didn't think so. The kids weren't really allowed in AJ's office, as a rule. Not because it was pervy or anything, but because the room was literally a walk-in space with a foldout chair, and the chances of Dallas and Paige breaking something were right at one hundred percent.

"Well, anyway, that makes me want to meet him more. I'll see you, hopefully at dinner if that's okay."

"We'll be at the house. Be careful."

"You got it, honey. Bye."

She hung up, and Kyler ducked into the coffee shop, damn near frozen to death. Shit it was cold out there.

"Hey, Kyler. The usual?"

Lord, he was getting to where the baristas knew his name and his order. "Please. Cold as a witch's tit out there."

"Coming right up."

He hunted a table, but didn't see one, so he moved off to one side so he could put his damn bags down. They were dragging at his arms.

"Well, Kyler Hale! How are you?" One of the moms from 4-H—Kayla? Kyla? Katia?—came up, all fuzzy hood and fake eyelashes. "How's it going?"

"Good. Good. How are you doing?" He tried for a smile, even if he was running down the list of all the things he had to do still today before Henley showed up.

"Excellent. I've been doing my last-minute shopping while my mom has Mikala. Where's Paige?"

"With her bestie and his dad." He was grateful too. Austin was a trouper.

"Oh? Mikala says that she's friends with that little autistic boy. *So* sweet of her."

Autistic? Dallas?

No.

Antisocial? A little. Shy? Yep. So smart he was scary? God yes. But Dallas just needed a bit of encouragement to trust that someone wasn't going to come after him.

"He's not autistic." He kept his voice even, adding in a hint of surprise. These folks might think he was rodeo trash, but he knew how to be Western and make someone eat their words and think it was their idea. "But he sure needed a friend who believed in him."

"Good for her!" She put her hand on his arm. "She's a little sweetheart. So brave and caring. She must get that from her daddy."

"Uh, thanks." Was she batting her eyelashes at him? And man, she had some amazing false eyelashes going on. And those eyebrows. Henley called them lacquered.

"Here's your coffee, Mr. Kyler." The barista handed him his cup and a smile. "Enjoy."

"What are you drinking, Kyler? Something strong or sweet?"

"Strong today. Thanks, Hannah." He raised his cup to... Kayla. It was Kayla. "Well, I should..."

"Did you want to sit? I have a table over here."

His brain said no, but his frozen feet said yes. He needed thicker socks, dammit. And longies to wear under his jeans. Cotton was the damn death fabric, after all. "I appreciate it."

"No problem! Come bring your packages. You need someone to make sure you don't freeze."

"It is pretty raw out there." He was pretty sure she was flirting with him, but then, a lot of the moms involved in Paige's activities seemed that way, and they were just being nice. It was like, a thing here. He wasn't sure how to read people.

Not only that, but...hell, he was very busy dealing with AJ and Henley, with the kids. With all these changes.

He didn't need any bonus drama from random women.

"So what do you do for fun?" she asked when he was settled across from her.

"I hang out with my kid. I'm good friends with Dallas's dad, as well." That felt... dishonest, though it was true. But he hadn't discussed his relationship status with Austin yet as far as telling random mostly strangers. So he wasn't going to feel guilty. AJ had a right to decide who knew for himself.

"Ah. He writes romance novels—gay ones. How brave, don't you think?"

"I guess? He's gay, after all." He grinned, thinking what AJ would have to say about this whole thing.

"Yes, that's the rumor." She chuckled, and the sound wasn't cruel. "Are you two...I mean, I don't want to be barking up the wrong tree."

"I'm not in the market." That was the best way to put it, right? He had an ex he co-parented with and a new boyfriend who was becoming a live-in. He was as taken as it got.

"Oh." Her face fell, but she didn't get pissy. "Well, good to know. We'll just have to be friends. What did you get Paige for Christmas? Mine wanted a dollhouse."

"Oh, Lord, my girl wanted all sorts of stuff for her horse, some books so she could catch up with Dallas on her reading, a new pair of boots, and chickens." Not necessarily in that order. He was happy to be friends. Hell, he could use a few.

"Chickens? Oh, how fun! What kind? We have silkies and Plymouth Rocks at the house. I want some that lay colored eggs."

"What do you recommend for first-timers?" he asked, grabbing his coffee to take a sip. "We've never had a place we could have them."

"Rhode Island Reds. No question. They're good egg producers, they're exceptional with kids, and they're hardy." She rolled her eyes, the drama evident. "Just winterize your coop or wait for spring? They can die of hypothermia quick."

"I'll give her the coop for Christmas, and an IOU for spring chickens." That tickled him. "Spring chickens."

She giggled, slapping the table. "Nice."

"Thanks. I'm here all week."

"Let her research her chickens, and she can use it for her 4-H project."

"Mmm." He tried for noncommittal.

"What? What is that mmm?" She frowned slightly. "It sounds ominous."

"She's not sure she wants to stay in 4-H."

"Oh? It seems like such a good fit for her."

Kyler shrugged, his neck a little hot. "A couple of the kids have been kind of mean about her being a rodeo kid. Really hurt her feelings."

"What? Have you talked to Ron and Maria? That's not cool. That's not what 4-H is about."

"I haven't yet, no. Paige is still trying to decide if she wants me to, and I'm trying to walk the line between letting her make decisions and encouraging her to stand up for herself." He gave her a wry smile. "I loved 4-H."

"Oh, man. She's six. Six still needs a parent to step in. Ten? Twelve? Sure." Kayla shook her head, eyebrows drawing together. "But she's still just a little girl, you know? Don't let her grow up too fast."

"You think?" He was flying blind a lot of the time, and Henley was a huge proponent of letting Paige choose stuff.

"Yes. She wants structure at this age. Wants you to have her back."

"Okay, cool, then. I'll talk to Ron and Maria." They seemed like good folks.

"I think that's a great idea. They can't help, if they don't know. Paige deserves better."

"Thanks." He really appreciated her thoughts. AJ tended to lean toward the super protective, because Dallas was so damn bullied, so he'd told Kyler Paige should leave if she was uncomfortable, but Kyler thought she could benefit from 4-H and needed to stick it out.

"Sure, and if you find out that it was my girl being evil,

you let me know." Kayla shook her head, her lips pursed. "Mikala wasn't raised to be evil, and we'll have a discussion about acting like a human being. She's still recovering from losing her father."

"I'm sorry. I didn't want to ask..."

"It was an accident." She sighed. "And I miss him like a sore tooth. So does my girl."

"I bet. That sucks." She was a much better egg than he'd given her credit for, and Kyler was a little ashamed of himself.

"Yeah. You were my first flirt." Her lips tightened, and she blinked quick a couple three times before she held his gaze. "How'd I do?"

"Good. Really good, hon. I promise." He chuckled. "I'm on uneven ground myself. I've never dated a guy before." So much for not blurting it out.

"No? Well, I have. It's tough." She tilted her head. "But I can tell you, they like it when you're yourself. Guys get a ton of bad press, but...if you're *you*, and he likes that? It's best."

"Yeah. I think I get what you mean." He actually thought being with AJ was way easier than Henley had been as far as just... everyday stuff. And God knew, they were compatible in bed.

"So, are you ready for Christmas now? I keep thinking I am, and I keep finding more things."

They started chatting then about nothing, and Kyler thought he'd found himself a friend.

And honestly, by the time he headed back out into the cold, he figured he might be ready to take on Henley and Christmas and the whole nine yards.

Chapter Eighteen

Austin had met a lot of lover's exes before.

He'd just never met one who was a woman.

Henley breezed into the ranch house like she lived there, her arms full of bags. "Whew! That last twisty part of the road coming into town is always a bear! Paige, honey, come give me a kiss. Ky, can you go grab my duffel? And I'll need to pull around to unload the horses."

"I'll get you moved, and you can come help me unload." Kyler kissed her cheek, and took her keys and headed outside, even as Paige flew into her arms.

"Mommy! I'm glad you're here. I need you to meet my friend, Dallas. He's the best. He has his own room, even."

"Does he now?" Henley had dropped the bags, and hugged Paige tight and kissed her face several times with big, smacking kisses.

Henley was a lovely woman, a petite, curvy brunette with bright hazel eyes, a smattering of freckles, and a ready smile. She grinned over Paige's head at him, then shifted Paige to one arm with effortless strength and held out a hand. "You must be Austin."

"Yes, ma'am. Austin Williams. I'm Dallas's father."

"That's my Poppy! He writes books and we're going to a big party tomorrow night."

Austin nodded to Dallas, tickled to death that Dallas felt brave enough to say hello.

"And you must be Dallas." Henley set Paige down, then crouched to Dallas's level to shake his hand as well. "I'm super happy to meet you finally. And I heard about this party. Sounds like so much fun."

"I—"

Dallas glanced at Paige, at him, and he nodded, smiled.

Paige whispered, "She's so nice, I promise."

"I have a sweater with sparkly lights on it to wear."

"Oh, neat! That sounds so cool." Henley stood, smiling. "Okay, let me go see to my horses. You know how it is, honey."

"The animals have to come first," Paige recited.

"Yep. I'll be right back!" She chugged back outside, leaving Austin feeling like he'd been hit by a whirlwind.

"So, should we make coffee? Does someone want to set the table?" Everything was ready, it was staying warm for supper.

"Daddy likes coffee, even at supper," Paige said.

"I'll get silvers," Dallas chimed in. They were such good kids.

"Cool. Let's be all ready, huh?" He and Ky had gone for stew and bread and a green salad, so it was all simple. Easy. There was pie for later. Henley was so damn pretty...

He wasn't sure how Ky could possibly go from Henley to him. It just seemed...impossible.

"Poppy? Are you going to pour the water in the pot?"

"Huh? Oh. Yeah." He did, then grinned at the kids, who had the table half set, if a bit randomly.

"Water is important for the coffee," Paige informed him. "Water and grounds and sugar and milk."

"And cups," Dallas added.

"Right. Cups." Austin grabbed out coffee cups, and before long, he heard boots stomping on the porch, Kyler and Henley coming in on a wave of cold air.

"Whew! That is raw," Henley said, rubbing her arms.

"Coffee is making."

"Thanks, honey," Ky said, smiling.

"There's stew and bread, Mommy. You can sit next to me. I'll sit between you and Dal. Dal always sits with me."

"Well, friends should sit together, huh? You just show me where."

"Daddy sits there, and Mr. Austin sits there. I sit here, so here?" Paige pointed to a chair, and he wanted to protest that she could sit by Ky if she wanted, but she just pulled out the chair and plopped down. "Now, do y'all mind if I take off my boots? My feet are killing me. Then I can help."

"You put your boots there in the box, Mommy. Show her, Dal."

"Daddy Ky made it!" Dallas hurried over and lifted the lid for the huge shoe chest.

"Oh, look at that. That's clever." Henley glanced at Ky, her expression unreadable, but he just grinned.

"Thanks. Shoes and boots get gross here. There's a little warming pad underneath that helps keep stuff dry without cracking anything."

"And it's got a water wicking pad too, because whoa." He winked at Ky, because they'd had to experiment a little with that.

"That's amazing."

"I'll take them, Mommy." Paige took Henley's boots over.

"What can I do?" Henley stood to go wash up at the sink.

"Take the salad to the table?" he suggested, when Ky didn't say anything. "I'll spoon up bowls of stew."

"You got it."

When he turned with the stew, Ky was watching him, those blue eyes as clear as a summer day, and just as hot.

He grinned, a little confused, a little turned-on, and a little buzzed. "Get the bread?"

"Sure, honey." Ky got the bread out of the warmer, then put butter on the table. He bumped hips with Austin on the way by, too.

Okay, so that felt pretty good. He approved. They all settled, and the kids chatted as they dug in.

Ky reached out under the table, stroking his thigh, touching him, nice and easy. He jumped a tiny bit, but then he had to grin. The touch grounded him. Made him feel like they were in this together. He was sitting here, next to Kyler, and Henley was down there.

"Poppy, did you know that my mom is famous?"

Austin nodded to Paige. "I did. She's a barrel racer. That's so cool."

Dallas glanced at Henley. "I don't have a mom. They made me in a lab. There was another lady who carried me inside her. But she's not my mom."

Henley sent Ky a panicked, wide-eyed 'oh help me'. And Ky chuckled and shook his head. "You have your poppy, though. And you have me and Paige."

Dallas grinned. "I do. My poppy wanted me. So bad. He paid all his money, just to have me."

"Families come in all sizes and shapes." That was the best that he had. Because he wasn't going to explain to a six-year-old that sometimes things didn't work out the way one wanted. He wasn't gonna explain he'd needed that baby. He'd wanted to be a father so badly. And he still did.

This was the best job ever, and he didn't regret a second. All the trouble and the cost and the loss. Because at the end, he got to know Dallas.

But no one could explain that to a six-year-old.

He wasn't sure he was gonna be able to explain that to a sixteen-year-old.

Paige beamed. "That's right. I have a momma and a daddy and a Penny. And a Dal."

Henley glanced at Kyler, kind of rolling her eyes a bit. "Do we always have such intense discussions around the supper table?"

"Oh yeah. We're into it."

"I detect no lies." Austin stifled a laugh, hiding his grin, although he was afraid his expression was a touch like a zombie's about to bite into somebody's brains. "I can't believe it's already fixing to be Merry Christmas."

Dallas bounced. "Santa comes in a couple of days. Poppy says Santa can come here, and he'll know where we are. We're gonna make cookies."

"Not today, though," Paige added. "Today we're hanging out with you, Mommy, and tomorrow is the party. Then it is Christmas Eve and cookies. And cocoa. And watching cartoons."

God, he hoped Ky had discussed all of this with Henley. Yeah, he didn't want to have to take Dallas home. All of the Christmas presents were here anyway. It didn't feel as if Henley was shocked or anything.

"I'm excited that we get to spend Christmas together. I'd like to stay even after your school starts. That way I get to meet your teacher."

"Me and Dal are in the same class." Paige lit up like a... Well, like a Christmas tree. "That's where I met him the very first day of school."

"Were you friends right away?" Henley asked.

Paige reared back a bit, shaking her head. "No. No, I made friends with Dal because somebody else wasn't very nice. We became best friends, though, because he's so cool."

Austin watched as his little boy shrank at the first part. And then sat up tall. And then taller again.

"He's really smart, and he thinks I'm smart, and he reads all the books. And he can do a walkover like it's nothing. Everybody thinks because he's a little skinny and he wears glasses that he's not cool. But he's so cool."

"Paige is my very best friend." Dallas managed to meet Henley's eyes. "I'm not like everybody else. Sometimes I can't breathe. Sometimes I get scared and don't want to answer the teacher. Even when I know the answer."

"Oh, honey." Henley clapped her hands and chuckled. "That happens to all of us. Every so often, I'll be fixing to ride. And I'll think, okay, I'm tired, I'm scared and I can't do it but the horse is ready, though, so we just go."

"That's what me and Paige do. Daddy Ky is teaching me how to be on a horse. I like the brushing part. Do you like to read?"

Henley's nose wrinkled before she could stop it. "Sometimes I like to read a romance."

Ky chuckled. "She listens to audiobooks on the drive sometimes."

"Really? Who's your favorite author?" Austin asked, forking up some salad.

"Oh, I like Lyla Sage," Henley said, her eyes lighting up.

"She has great covers," Austin agreed. "And a nice slow burn."

"Does that mean it takes them forever to kiss?" Dallas asked.

"That's it, kiddo."

"My Poppy writes romances. His boys always kiss, but sometimes they have to fight first, and sometimes they make Poppy cry when they fight."

"Do they?" Henley arched one perfectly lacquered eyebrow at him.

"It's a hazard of the job." If he didn't care enough to cry over them, how could he expect his readers to?

"We all have our sh-tuff, huh? With me, it's the horses. It kills me when one gets hurt."

"Oh, man. I bet." He couldn't imagine. "That's why we had to bring Mr. Mistoffelees here. I was worried about him being lonely all alone at the condo..."

"Mr. Mist—"

"Mr. Mistoffelees," Paige piped up. "He's a magical kitty, and he's black and white, and he is from a *show*!"

Dallas nodded. "He is black and white, and Poppy named him. Poppy loves kitties."

Henley glanced at Austin, and all he could do was smile. He was a cat guy. He liked dogs too. Birds. Hamsters.

Hell, he'd gone into the barn without Kyler to get the kids once, even. No one had trampled him, so he took that as a good thing.

"*Cats*. That's the show," Ky said.

Henley chuckled. "Okay, here's where I got to admit I haven't seen a musical since the ones they did in high school."

"Poppy showed us *Cats* and we are all going to see *The Lion King* in Denver!" Dallas clapped, so excited. "We're going to stay in a fancy hotel and everything."

"I have a book signing, and we're making a long weekend of it," Austin explained, and Henley gave Ky another one of those long, searching stares.

What did that even mean?

He knew that Ky had told Henley they were together, right? His cat was living here now.

His son had his own room.

"That sounds really nice," Henley said finally.

Ky grinned, his cheeks a little pink. "Yeah. I hear there are great big puppets that look like giraffes, right, Paige?"

"And elephants! And antelopes!"

"We are going to have so much fun!" Dallas stood, rolled into a handstand and wiggled, making Paige giggle.

"No gymnastics at supper, son."

"Sorry." He plonked back into his seat.

Henley had a nice laugh, low and throaty. "That was an impressive handstand, though, honey."

"Momma can do that on a horse," Paige piped up.

"Ow, wow, can we see?"

"If the horses are feeling good, I'll saddle up my mare and show you tomorrow." Henley winked, magnanimous as hell.

"It depends on the snow. You don't want your momma to freeze, do you? She's a Texan, remember." The tease sounded familiar, well-practiced.

"She'll be a block of ice," Paige agreed.

"Brrrr." Henley grinned wide at Austin, inviting him to play, he thought, not pushing him out.

It was incredibly sweet.

"No freezing the cowgirl."

Dallas's eyes went wide. "No. Oh, no. I wouldn't freeze you. You're Paige's mommy."

"We'll see then, how it goes." Henley ate some more stew, making a yum face. "Y'all, this is good."

Austin grinned at Ky. "We made it together. We're a solid pair."

"It looks like it. I can make two things, right, niblet?"

Paige giggled. "Naner pudding and King Ranch casserole."

"What's a king rancherole?" Dallas asked, eyes wide. "Does it have a crown?"

Austin felt his chuckles trying hard to bubble up.

"It's a casserole, kiddo. Like lasagna or chicken and broccoli." Ky waved a hand. "It's named after a ranch in Texas."

"Rancherole sounds like more fun, though, doesn't it? Like a casserole served on a throne or with pretty diamonds on the top."

Paige started waving her spoon around. "Ooh...or rancheroli! Like ravalamaolis from a can!"

He shook his head, because kids were amazing.

Ky grabbed some bread and buttered it, looking on with a proud grin.

Soon the kids were making up a nonsense ravioli casserole with diamonds song, and Henley was staring at them like they were both insane.

That was okay. She'd get used to them.

Sooner or later she would have to, right?

"When did she get silly?" Henley asked, careful not to be heard. "She never was before."

"It's great, huh?" Kyler's answer was a nonanswer, but he kinda liked it.

"It's amazing." Henley focused on Austin, and grinned to beat the band, even if there was a hint of bitter in it. "She needed this. A friend. A home. I knew she did."

"She's amazing. I love her dearly, and I will never be able to repay her for what's she's done for Dallas." That was the god's honest truth. He loved Ky, but he would lay down his life for Paige, just like he would for Dallas.

Ky squeezed his leg. "I'm pretty happy about it too."

"Can we go play, Daddy?" Paige stood up. "We're doing a puzzle, Mommy. Want to help?"

"Sure, kiddo. Put your dishes in the sink. Gently, please."

He and Ky had been forced to put a dish towel in the bottom of the sink because it was one of those ceramic farmhouse sinks, and the kids could reach to drop their dishes in.

Fashion over function, Kyler complained all the time.

"I'll be in there after a bit, baby. I want the tour and to see my room and everything."

They had four bedrooms—theirs, the kids', and a guest room, which was amazing, because they had bonus room for an office for them to share. He kind of loved it, and his clothes hung in the closet next to Kyler's, his socks and unders rested in the dresser next to Kyler's.

He felt like part of something bigger than himself and Dallas.

"So, Daddy Kyler?" One of her eyebrows lifted. "That's pretty serious."

"Yeah." Kyler met his gaze again for a moment. "It is. I feel good about it."

"I do too. I like being a family."

"Well, I'm so tickled." Henley took her dishes to the sink. "Let me help with this, and then y'all can give me the tour."

Okay, then. That was easier than he'd feared. He wanted this, in a scary intense way. Kyler made him trust in things he needed to believe in.

Chapter Nineteen

The party was... well, it sure wasn't what Kyler expected from a ranch Christmas to-do.

This was fancy, even as it was kid-friendly and family-oriented. And there were lots of glittery folks.

Famous ones. Actors and singers and shit. He recognized a lot of them, and it made his feet itch in his good boots, made his jacket feel tight across his shoulders.

Even Henley, who was famous in her own right, was a little shell-shocked to see Paige playing with the daughter of an Oscar winner.

AJ had introduced him to Stoney and Ford, who owned the place. Ford was fancy too, but Stoney seemed like a cowboy, like a logical type.

But even then, no one seemed worried about kissing each other, holding hands. He'd never seen anything like it.

He wasn't... mad at it. But it felt as if he was standing in someone else's world. And Austin had been dragged away by a couple of writers, the kids off playing with the seemingly hundreds of dogs...

So he was like the proverbial sore thumb.

"Hello there, handsome. Would you like a drink?" This well-coifed dude in a sparkly sweater offered him a martini glass of something bright red.

"Uh. Sure." That would give him something to do with his hands. Right? "Thank you."

"You're welcome. I'm Dean. I'm an art director at the Flying Diamond agency. We format Austin's books for him."

"Oh. Well, pleased to meet you, Dean. I'm Kyler." He moved his glass to his left hand to hold out his right to shake.

"Kyler Hale, hmm? I knew you had to be when I saw you. I think it's amazing that Austin is together with his cover model. Are you available for more shoots?"

His mouth went dry, and he couldn't figure out what to say for a moment. Then he cleared his throat. "Uh—"

"No, hmm? Shame. I'm going to have to speak sternly to Austin. Very sternly."

"You are? Why?" He blinked, trying to figure out what was going on here.

"Keeping you all to himself, of course. I could keep you wickedly busy, but I understand." Dean chuckled softly. "This is my favorite party all year. We like the gay ski week and Easter, and the big summer party is gorgeous, but this one's special."

"It's sure pretty." He felt like he was missing half the conversation. "The kids are really happy."

"Have you met Geoff and Tiny? They're the kitchen staff. That little bitty girl is their grandbaby, Ivy."

Austin knew folks with staff.

Austin was friends with folks with staff.

"Um. No. No, I'll have to meet them." Maybe he could escape to the kitchen for a breather.

"You'll recognize them — Tiny is a bear, and Geoff is a little rainbow-haired twink-looking guy."

A bear. That was... okay. "Sure. Excuse me?" He almost ran for the kitchen.

The kitchen was outside, and he passed a couple making out in the shadows. "Oh. Sorry. Sorry."

"No worries." The low chuckle had his cheeks burning, and he caught his heel in the sidewalk, damn near going ass over teakettle.

"Oops." Firm arms caught him. "Got you. Are you hunting for something? I'm Stoney and Ford's son, and I can help."

"I was trying to duck into the kitchen. I—" He swallowed. "Sorry."

"Sure. Sure, not problem. It's this way. Are you hunting for something gluten-free? Vegan? Or just the best coffee?"

"Coffee. Definitely coffee." That red drink had been... whoa.

"It's the best when Geoff makes it. Seriously." The kid led him through the snow and up to a brightly lit door.

"Thanks. I appreciate it. I'm Kyler."

"Quartz. This is Tiny and Geoff. Geoff, Mr. Kyler would like a fancy coffee."

"Oh? Latte? Cappuccino?" That was some bright hair. "Kyler...you belong with Austin, hmm? He's such a sweetheart."

"He is." He was, but he knew all these people... "Can I just have a coffee?"

"Of course." Geoff's head tilted. "Honey, are you okay? Come in. Come in and sit. You're pale as a ghost."

"Thanks. I'm not sure I'm cut out for fancy parties." In fact, he knew he wasn't.

"Oh, us neither. It's way more fun in the kitchen." Tiny—who was huge, by the way—winked at him. "I will say, by and large, these folks are kind and solid. Some of them are even... normal."

"Never say so!" Geoff swatted Tiny's butt, like it was nothing.

"How did y'all meet Austin?"

"He did a book signing up here. It was adorable. He had all his books, posters—his fans showed up. Some even came from out of town and stayed up here. I think the bosses are having him do another one when his new book comes out. Do you get to read them first?"

"I haven't yet, no." His cheeks heated painfully.

"Well, I'm jealous that you get to be any part of the process. I've read all his books. I cried when Maverick was done."

"I- yeah. I mean, I like the books a lot." He was starting to feel a little hunted.

A coffee was sat in front of him, and Tiny touched Geoff's hand as he went back to cooking.

"Do you want cream or sugar?" Tiny asked.

"No. No, thanks. I'm sorry to be in your way." His voice cracked. What the fuck was wrong with him? He'd spent years on the road, scraping by and damn near losing fingers in the roping pen when he wasn't riding, and he couldn't handle a freaking party?

"You're fine. Seriously. You can hang out here. No stress." Geoff gave him a warm smile. "Seriously. You're welcome."

"Thanks." He sat and sipped his coffee, and he tried to figure out what had him so freaked out. Was it the lack of a clear idea of how he and AJ were presenting themselves together? Was it the cover art thing? Was it just not really being out, so to speak?

Was it knowing that he was way more comfortable in this kitchen than he was ever going to be out there with the people Austin was with?

He took a deep breath. Okay. Right. He should probably go at least check in. Make nice. These were Austin's friends.

"Thanks for the coffee, y'all."

"Of course. We're looking forward to meeting you again." Geoff offered him what felt like a worried smile.

"Stay warm," Tiny called.

"I will." Kyler headed back out, determined to be brave.

Henley was laughing when he walked in, her pretty sweater sparkling in the lights. "Kyler! Kyler, have you met Jonas here? He saw me ride at the finals."

"That's great, honey." He shook hands with the man, who he recognized as one of the country music singers doing the rodeo circuit. "She's a hell of a barrel racer."

"Yes, sir. She's amazing, and your little girl is amazing." Jonas smiled at Henley, the expression a little too warm for his liking. "She said y'all came with Austin Williams?"

"We did." Lord, did everyone in this crowd know Austin?

"He's a sweetheart. He signed a book for my mom."

Someone's mom read Austin's gay books? That was wild.

Henley giggled. "That's awesome."

"I—yeah." Someone's mom had a book with his belly on it.

Jonas frowned at him, and Henley tilted her head. "Are you okay? You seem pale. Jonas, honey, can you please go grab Austin for me?"

"Sure. Of course." Jonas hightailed it, and she studied him.

"What is it?"

"I'm just really wigging out, Hen."

"Why? What is it?"

"What is it? Look at this place!" he hissed, careful to keep his voice down. "It's full of out-and-proud fancy gay people, and Austin is friendly with them. Austin belongs with these people, not with me."

"Kyler? Babe?" A warm hand landed on his arm. "What's wrong?"

People were starting to pay attention to them.

He backed off, crossing his arms over his chest. "Sorry. Sorry, I—" He tried to think of what he wanted to say.

"What's wrong? Can I get you a drink? They have this Santa martini thing..."

"Oh, yeah. It's kinda foul." He made a face, trying for funny.

"Is it? Figures. I didn't try it." Austin wrinkled his nose. "I've got a fake ginger ale. I mean, it's a real ginger ale. It's fake booze, you know, because I was keeping an eye on the kids."

"I took a sip. Then I escaped to the kitchen to have coffee."

Henley stepped back, and he wanted to call her a coward as she moved out of earshot.

"Lucky! Geoff makes the best coffee. He makes a hazelnut latte to die for." AJ reached for his hand.

He pulled back a little, and Austin's eyebrows flew up. "Kyler, what's wrong?"

He glanced around at all the glittery folks. "I don't want to go into it here."

"O-okay...Miss Henley, can you please watch Dallas and Paige for a second?"

"Sure, Austin." Henley gave Austin a sad smile. "No problem."

"Come on. There's a little dressing room back here." Austin put his hands in his pockets and headed toward a door in the back.

Kyler followed, feeling miserable as hell for disappointing Austin and Henley both. Jesus, he was a fucking mess.

Austin led him into a tiny room, turned on a light and glanced at him, face a study in confusion. "What on earth did I do?"

"I—It's me, Austin. It's totally me. I just—" He waved a hand. "This whole thing. I don't belong here. I'm pretty sure I can't do this."

Austin tilted his head like he was hearing a whistle. "Can't do what? Go to a party?"

"The party is just a symptom." Kyler paced the tiny room, back and forth. "I'm not— Honey, I don't fit in with these folks. I don't know what to say to them. I keep panicking."

"They're only people. I mean, they have way, way more money than I do, but they're decent people, I swear."

"I know that." He blew out a sigh. "But they're— I mean, they all know you. You were right in there, smiling and laughing, and I couldn't even string two damn words together."

"They all know a writer. It's my job. I lie for a living."

"You—" He blinked at that. "What does that even mean?"

"What? I make shit up for a job — it's not just characters. I have to show up as Austin Williams, queer romance author. You were in the public eye, for fuck's sake. It's not any different, is it?"

"I—" Was it? Henley had fans here. He got recognized at the feed store... "I guess it's not, no."

"I would feel as out of place at the Cattleman's Ball, Kyler."

That had him blinking again. "You would?" He wasn't trying to be an ass. He was trying to understand what was going on with him. Why he was so damn miserable and making a fuss.

"Yeah. I'd have to watch what I said, not tell anyone what I wrote, not touch your back, not call you babe, and manage that while being charming and social." Austin met his eyes, deadly serious. "I have to lie all the time, you know. I hid being queer as a kid. When I became a single dad, I hid being terrified because I had a sick baby and no support. I have to worry about the political climate, global warming, and whether peanut butter causes autism. When I decided to write for a living, I had to hide the worry that no one would buy my books, that the ideas would dry up, that I was too gay, not gay enough, not social enough, not extroverted enough. I have to watch and not let people see that I have a condo because one of my ex's friends feels sorry for me and charges me pennies on the dollar. I have to pretend that everything is okay when I don't have health insurance or I can't buy food because one of the distributors didn't pay or I have to hire someone to be a cover model so I can restart a series!"

Kyler's mouth dropped open. Then snapped shut. Then opened again.

He felt like one of those ventriloquist dummies.

"Austin—"

AJ shook himself, then straightened his shoulders, that mask of calm dropping down again. "We can't leave until Santa comes for the kids, but that shouldn't be long, then we can go. I'm sorry about the party. I thought it would be a good opportunity."

"Wait, what?" That was two different lines of thought, but he seized on the first one. "Why are you leaving?"

"You are uncomfortable and want to go?" AJ's brows furrowed and a want line showed up in the center of his forehead.

"Oh!" He wanted to smack himself. "You mean the party. I— shit. I thought you meant at the house, honey. You scared the fucking fire out of me."

Austin's eyes went wide, and all the color leached from the angular face. "I—No. No, are we...I mean, this isn't a fight, is it?"

"No." There was no question mark at the end of that for him. "But I am being an ass. I can't seem to help it." Kyler raked his hand through his hair. "I freaked out, and then even the guys in the kitchen seemed to be pointing out how I didn't belong here, honey."

"Nonsense. Stoney? The co-owner? He inherited this place from his son's grandfather. He's a ranch cowboy. He's working, just like I am. If you asked him, he'd rather be riding. I thought...well, he needs saddles, and he meets tons of folks, and he's happy to give the community work."

"You're amazing." How could he have let that be less than the most important thing? This was about him and AJ, not about other folks. "One on one I'm sure I'd be fine, but we haven't even talked about..." He waved a hand again. "Us. Like what us is to other folks."

"I get that."

"What?" Okay, that was—unexpected.

"The first time I was in a queer space—like an open queer space?—I was freaked. I was jealous, I felt like people were speaking a different language, like everyone was so overt because I'd been so deep in the closet. I—I was in college, so I guess I didn't think." AJ took his hand again, squeezed his fingers. "I'm sorry that you're nervous. Want to hang out with me? I'll introduce you to Stoney, and I promise not to desert you again."

How had...

AJ gave everything to him. Just here—you need this, I'll give it. Kyler had misread the fuck out of everything, including how vulnerable his man was, and AJ kept loving on him.

"Yes." He could do that. They would have to talk. He knew it. There was a ton to unpack, but they had to get through tonight first, and their kids were out there waiting for party Santa. "Please?"

AJ beamed at him and offered him an arm. "Shall we, then? And we'll ask for ginger ale in pint glasses?"

"You got it."

Kyler could do this if Austin was with him. They had each other's backs.

And that was the way he was going to navigate this whole damn thing from now on.

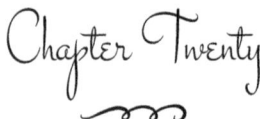

Chapter Twenty

Austin had a vicious headache. He'd not been able to sleep, so he finally gave it up and went to work. He finished a couple of chapters on the new book.

He had no idea if they would be word salad when he woke up, but last night they'd seemed okay, and they'd gone quick, and it was better than trying to sleep when he couldn't.

Last night had been weird. Austin kind of felt as if Ky thought Austin Williams, author, was who he actually was and that didn't make any sense.

He hadn't even tried to be his public persona, not the whole time that they'd been together.

So, yeah, that was weird.

Then of course, he'd lost his shit in a major goddamn way, which was glorious because there was nothing like saying, "Oh, well, by the way, I'm not near as successful as I'd like to be, or that I pretend to be," in front of your lover and also the person he wanted to impress the most in the whole world.

That had been great.

Not only that, but it had been late, and it had been

Christmas Eve-Eve. At least until it turned Christmas Eve after midnight.

So it wasn't as if he could have gotten anybody online to complain or to vent or to try to explain how he was a big faker.

And worst of all, what if Ky thought that was who he really was.

"Hey, Austin, honey." Henley bumped him gently with her shoulder as she walked into the kitchen. "Is it all right if I take the kids down into town? I thought I'd let them do some last-minute shopping, and then I'd grab some pizzas to bring up. You know, pizza seems to be like a Christmas Eve sort of thing. Pizzas and jammies and color books and comics."

He found her a smile, even if it felt off. "Oh that would be very sweet. Dallas would love that."

She grinned back at him, her curls kind of bobbing as she nodded. "I had fun last night, thanks for inviting me. I might even have a date for New Year's Eve."

"Wow, did you meet someone?" That was fast.

"I did. And maybe— Yeah, maybe he says he could fly me out to his concert in LA for New Year's Eve and then we could party. Then he could fly me back."

"Sounds perfect." And fancy.

He was kind of curious as to what Paige would think about getting dumped for a guy, but that was none of his business. Austin wasn't dumping Dal and Paige for money or fame or for a hot guy. Those kids were his priority.

Not that Ky wasn't hot...

"It is." She chuckled. "But he's nice."

"Nice is great. If you happen to find any penuche fudge while you're out, could you hook me up?"

"Totally. No problem." She met his eyes, her nose wrinkling a little bit. "He really likes you, you know. Yesterday was hard."

"I'm sorry that it was. I didn't intend to put him in that situation."

"He needed to be in the situation. If he's gonna be with a guy, he's going to have to admit he's queer. It's a thing. He doesn't have to say he's gay, but if he's in a relationship with you? He has a daughter, and he's going to have to explain it. I mean, Dallas knows you're gay, yes?"

"Yeah, of course." There wasn't any reason to lie. It wasn't as if Austin had really dated yet, except for Ky, but Dallas was aware he wasn't going to have a mom, and there wasn't ever going to be a girlfriend. Austin had a lot of gay friends who had kids.

"So, he has to get used to things if this — if you are who he wants. He doesn't have to go out and wave the flag at the Pride parade, but he doesn't have to lie. It's important. Paige deserves to see that he's not ashamed."

What was he supposed to say? Thank you? Fuck. "Paige is tickled that you're here sharing the holiday."

That was innocuous.

"I wanted to. I miss her you know? But I'm just... I don't live a life that's kid-friendly. I figure in ten years I'm going to be the coolest mom around, but until then? When she can spend the summer with me riding the circuit and having a ball? Until then, she needs a stable home and school and friends and her daddy." He got one of those teasing winks. "And her poppy."

"I promise to be good to her."

She snorted. "I know. Kyler wouldn't be with you if you weren't. Full stop."

"No. No, you're right." Ky was all about Paige and her happiness and safety. They had that in common.

"I am. I'll be back with pizza and fudge and goodies." She squeezed his shoulder. "The kids are out with Ky. I'll have him load them up."

"Sure. If Dallas needs to ask me, I'm good with it."

"Cool." She floated away, and he headed into the kitchen for a glass of water and a Tylenol.

It wasn't long before he heard her vehicle chug out of the yard, and then Ky was there, grabbing a Coke out of the fridge, staring at him.

"What's wrong?" What was he looking at?

"Nothing, honey. I don't want you to be mad at me." Kyler's little grin was wry as hell.

"I'm not." He was confused, worried, uncertain, embarrassed, stressed, and feeling like a moron, but he wasn't mad.

"I can work with that." Ky watched him take his Tylenol. "Merry Christmas Eve."

"Merry Christmas Eve. Are we okay?" He didn't feel okay.

"I think so, yeah." Ky sighed. "Come sit with me, honey. Let's iron this out?"

He grabbed his water and went to the huge kitchen table, trying his dead-level best not to freak out.

Kyler sat across from him. "I'm sorry about last night, AJ. I should have just come to you and said I was worried. I've never had a panic attack in my life, but I was damn close last night, and I lost my shit."

"I'm so sorry that you were uncomfortable. I didn't intend for you to be. Thanks for telling me, though. I'm glad I eased you a little bit."

"You did." Ky rubbed his jaw, the scrape of stubble loud. Someone hadn't shaved this morning. "And I'm sorry I upset you. You seemed so comfortable, and I was miserable, and I jumped to conclusions. And got to having imposter syndrome." Ky shot him a sheepish glance. "I looked it up last night, late. You...you hide it, honey. Better than anyone."

"It's my job." He tried hard not to let it show, to act like he was so sure...

"I know, but I guess I bought it." Ky chuckled. "I mean,

the only thing you seem less than sure about sometimes is Dallas and how you should be raising him."

"I could say the same for you, cowboy. You exude confidence."

"Well, I'm full of shit," Kyler told him. "I mean, I'm glad it didn't happen because of a lot of reasons, but to begin with the reason I didn't marry Henley is because a shit ton of her friends and family told me I wasn't good enough for her. That I would drag her down on her way to the NFR."

"Nonsense." But it didn't matter even if it was. "Are you in love with her, still?"

"No." Ky shook his head firmly. "No way. It was never more than best friends with benefits, and I couldn't fall any harder for you than I have. Or at least I thought so until last night. When you yelled at me? I knew I was a goner."

"I—What?" He didn't follow. "What does that mean?"

"It means you care enough to fight with me. To tell me I don't know it all. That I can be wrong. That's a good thing, honey. I mean, I'm not one to tie it up, but if we're too lukewarm to stand up to each other, this is never gonna work." Ky's eyes blazed blue fire at him.

"I feel a lot of things about you, Ky. Lukewarm isn't one of them."

"Yeah." Ky tilted his head. "You know you can move in, right? You don't have to keep paying for the condo."

"I didn't want to—" His cheeks burned, and he had to swallow so he didn't choke on his stress. "It's not about the money. I am making it."

He wasn't setting the world on fire, but he was making it.

"Well, no. It's not about money. You live here pretty much already, and I don't give two shits about your money." Ky reached out to grab his hand. "I want you and Dal here."

"You already have my cat..." He twined their fingers

together. "And I'm stupid in love with you. But...I have to warn you, Kyler. I'm gay."

"I know." Ky squeezed his hand. "And I know it's wrong to ask you not to be. Which I wouldn't do. I need to get my head around us and how to be an us. I never even did that with Henley, really."

"Well, tell me what you need, because...I don't want to lose you, but I can't go back to hiding." And if Ky needed that, they'd have to...not.

"I need you to be patient. I want to be with you. Be a couple." Ky chuckled. "I have to learn how, and I can't promise there won't be more freaking out." Then he turned serious. "What I can promise is to talk to you from now on."

"Please. I know it's a new world—a new language, a new culture, everything—but I can help you navigate it." Now that he knew what was worrying Ky, he could help. "And I know that Stoney was tickled to meet you."

Hell, Stoney had even taken Kyler aside for a quiet chat.

"He was fantastic, honey. He said he'd been going through my portfolio online, and he offered to put a piece of art in the lobby at the ranch for me to advertise with."

"Oh, wow. So cool."

Ky's cheeks heated, the pink so cute. "And he ordered half a dozen saddles with the ranch brand on them."

"Oh, dude! Dude, you'll be busy as hell." He applauded, tickled to death. This was what he'd hoped for Ky. Stoney had real connections.

"I will. So thank you. It was a wonderful opportunity, even if they did all think I was a weirdsmobile."

"No one said so. They all thought you were hot..." And his. They were all jealous.

He had the cover cowboy.

"How weird is that? As long as you think I'm hot, then I'm happy." Kyler's gaze went wicked. "The kids are gone."

"They are…we're all alone, and we're together in your house…"

"*Our* house."

Oh, that made his heart happy. "Our house."

"And we can go be in our bedroom without anyone knowing." Ky stood so fast his chair skidded. He held out his hand, and Austin took it, letting Ky pull him to his feet so they could practically run to the bedroom.

Kyler did close the bedroom door behind them, just in case, but then he got busy stripping AJ's clothes off. They'd done a lot of sleeping together. A lot of quick hand and mouth stuff. But this? They had time. And he wanted to do it up right.

So he started with that oversized sweater. "You're so fucking hot, honey. I see those collarbones peeking and it's such a tease."

He loved the way AJ blushed.

"I'm not a tease. Right?" AJ let his hands hang at his sides, and Kyler looked his fill.

"No. God, no, honey. You're wonderful." He tugged the T-shirt off too. "You make my mouth dry. I—I'd like to make love to you. You interested?"

"It's been a long time. I'm more than interested. I'm in."

He waggled his eyebrows. "I think it goes the other direction…"

Austin laughed. "I'm easy. Pitching. Catching. I just want you."

His cock, which was half hard, surged to full against his zipper placket. Whoa. "I want you too."

He wanted to explore Austin's body, feel how tight Austin would be all around his cock.

It made his eyes cross a little.

AJ tugged at his shirt. "You too, babe."

"Huh? Oh." Right. Clothes. He bared his chest, but then he had to pause to take the kiss that he needed.

AJ worked his belt open, fighting his jeans off and down over his hips and legs.

He stepped out of them, then pushed at AJ's. doing the same until they fell naked on the bed together. He rolled AJ beneath him, his hands on Austin's cheeks, his lips finding his lover's again.

The kisses liked to burn him, AJ's hard cock rubbing alongside his own. "Don't stop."

"No chance." He hummed deep in his throat, pressing down to get more friction as he nibbled at Austin's jaw and neck. He had lube. Condoms. But he was distracted by the salt of Austin's skin, by the way he arched and rocked.

That sweet prick was leaving burning kisses on his belly, and it was driving him crazy. He reached between them, stroking them together.

"Uhn!" AJ shook, staring into his eyes. "Not gonna last if you keep doing that."

"Then I need to try to get the lube." He kissed AJ until they were both breathless.

"Mmhmm. You should totally do that. I'll watch."

"Okay." He laughed, because the air was pretty cold, so he grabbed the lube and condoms and dove back under the comforter to wrap around Austin again.

AJ pushed right into his arms. "Have I mentioned how much I love our bed?"

"I'm glad." He loved AJ in it. He kissed and licked and sucked all the skin he could reach. "I want you right here."

"I'm going to lose my mind, babe. I want you in me. I want you to remind me that I'm sexy."

"You so are."

"I'm a long, tall drink of water with a big Adam's apple."

Kyler hooted. "But you're my long, tall drink of water." He nipped at that Adam's apple. "Okay. See me not fumble the lube and be all suave."

"If you do, I'll wait to tease you about it until tomorrow."

"No sex teasing on Christmas." It was a rule, right?

"Oh, right. Boxing Day then."

"Okay, deal." He knew Boxing Day from listening to AJ read stories to the kids. He popped the lube open, only wasting a tiny bit as he squeezed too hard. Then he got his fingers wet, because he wanted this to be good, not painful.

When AJ bent one knee and let him in, it was the single most erotic moment of his life. He gritted his teeth against the need to come as his balls pulled up, and Kyler breathed deep, in and out.

Then he pressed a finger against Austin's entrance. The ring of muscles gripped him, and he had to groan. He had no choice.

"Mmm...that's so good, babe..."

"It is." He sank his finger inside AJ, and he was so hot. So smooth. Tight. God, his dick was going to just explode.

Austin began to rock, fucking himself in slow, gentle rolls, driving him nuts.

"Tell me when you—"

"Give me more, Kyler. Stretch me good."

So he nodded, breathless and eager, and slid another finger inside AJ's body.

There was no way he was going to fit.

No way. It was impossible.

"Come on, babe. I'm not made of glass."

"You're too tight."

AJ laughed. "Not too tight for you."

"Promise?"

"Who's the expert-level gay?"

He snorted, because that was exactly what he needed to hear. That *someone* knew what they were doing. "Don't let me hurt you."

"I won't. It's a deep burn, and I'll feel you everywhere. You're going to make me ache."

"Lube me up?" He was selfish enough to want to feel Austin's hand on him. He needed it, in fact. Even if it would strain his damn control.

"Oh, I can do that." AJ slicked his fingers, dragging them over his shaft, teasing his cockhead. He took the torture as long as he could, his heart throbbing, his cock aching.

Then he reared back, ready to settle himself between Austin's legs. "Now, honey?"

"Now. Please, my love. Please, fuck me."

"Now," he agreed, pressing down and forward, slow and sure. He knew this part, knew how to wait until AJ adjusted, then slide in to the root.

It was tighter than any fist, and his body insisted that he was going to burst into flames. AJ's near-black eyes bored into him, the hunger a visible thing.

"Love." He thrust, moving slowly at first, then faster as Austin wrapped around him and tugged.

"Uh-huh."

"Need you so damn much."

"I'm yours. Don't stop. Please." AJ gasped for him, his lover not silent at all.

All those little sighs and moans made him move faster, his ass clenching, his spine tingling from the strain of holding back. "Soon, honey. Soon."

AJ bore down, squeezing him hard enough that he slammed in, scrabbling for a handhold on Austin's cock. Austin's fingers met him there, and together they stroked until Austin shouted, the sound ringing off the rafters as he came.

And Kyler slid home one more time, joining him in his release.

His balls ached, throbbing as they emptied, and all he could do was rock there on his hands and knees.

Then AJ eased him down gently, kissing him, and he tried not to squash Austin too bad. Though Austin had him beat for size...

"Mmm...best Christmas Eve ever." AJ nuzzled his jaw. "Love you. I said that, right?"

"You did. And I love you too, honey. So much. Thank you for hanging in there." He kissed Austin's neck. "I'm going to make you happy, and I'm going to raise children with you."

"I want that so much." Kyler held him close. "Almost as much as I wanted to be alone with you."

AJ laughed, kissing his nose. "Well, we do have a while yet..."

"We do at that." Cuddling first.

Then he would see if he was up to anything else on Christmas Eve.

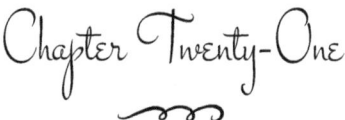

Chapter Twenty-One

"Poppy! Poppy, wake up. Santa Claus came!"

Austin checked to make sure both he and Ky had shorts on. Then he lifted the comforter and grabbed Dallas, yanking him under it with giant growling and chomping noises.

"Eeee! Paige. Save me!"

"Dal! I'm coming!" Paige careened into the room, looking around with wild eyes.

"Arrrrr nom nom nom!" Kyler snarled and darted out to pull Paige in.

"Nooooo!" Paige giggled, though, her struggling patently fake.

"Grr!" He hugged Dallas tight. "Santa Monster!"

"Monnnnnster!"

"What the Sam hell is going on here?" Henley asked from the doorway of the bedroom. When he peeked out of the covers, he found her wearing a Mrs. Claus apron and two oven mitts.

"Uh, Hen, if you're cold, we have blankets," Ky said. "No need to steal kitchen gear."

"Ha-ha. I am making blueberry muffins. From a mix," she admitted.

"Yum." Austin popped his head out of the covers. "The blanket monsters have eaten the kids, so more for us."

"Poppy!" Dallas wiggled out from under his arm. "I like muffins."

"Me too." Paige emerged, her hair sticking up all over with static. "And pressies!"

"After muffins and some coffee for me and Daddy," Austin said.

"Come on, you two. You can help me get plates and butter and stuff," Henley said, winking. "Merry Christmas, guys."

"Mmm." They all trooped out, and Ky grabbed him for a kiss. "Morning. Merry Christmas."

"Morning, babe. Merry Christmas to you." Austin held on tight, rocking them together. "She's not going to poison us, is she?"

"Uhhh... Not if it's a mix. She can follow directions."

Lord help him.

Not that either one of them was appreciably better.

The Christmas tree was packed full with gifts — books and clothes and toys and sleds and new bikes for both kiddos. It was the kind of Christmas he'd dreamed of giving Dallas, with a sibling and a ton of love and happy music and...

He took a deep breath. "Should we put on the matching jammies?"

"God, yes. This is going to be a hoot."

They dressed in their Thing One and Thing Two jammies, and their elf shoes with bells on the toes. Hand-in-hand, they wandered together to the front room, where the smell of coffee and baking muffins greeted them.

Yum.

"Oh my god, y'all. You two crack me up." Henley snorted,

pouring them both a mug of coffee. "I let the kids have their stockings."

"Without us?"

"No, like right now. They're waiting for you to open them."

"Oh, cool." Ky tugged him to the couch. "You have a timer on, right?"

"I do. We have twenty minutes. Let's do this." Henley bounced, plopping on the couch across from the kids.

The children ripped into their stockings, oohing and ahhing at the small toys, crayons, and oranges and apples. Paige and Dallas each got a gift card from his parents and Henley's, which Austin melted over.

Henley's people were more than willing to fold Dallas into their goofy huge family too.

"Poppy, look! A tiny book!" Dallas showed him a mini book, the kind that came with little toys attached. It was Sherlock Holmes, and it had a magnifying glass on the string.

"From Santa, huh?"

"Oh, that's cool..." Paige examined the book with a hint of a frown, then Dallas nudged her.

"You have to have one too. Santa is fair."

"Hmm." She dug in her stocking and pulled out a bitty wrapped package. "Oooh!" She tore it open, gently for her, and blinked. "It's about horses! Oh, wow! Mommy, I got a horsey book!"

Henley applauded. "Y'all are going to both have to read to me!"

"Okay! After we color?"

"Sounds great." The timer went off, and Henley went to save breakfast while the kids settled in with crayons and color books. That meant they could have coffee.

Thank God.

He leaned against Ky, breathing nice and slow. All the big

gifts were out here, but the signed copy of *The Joy of Gay Sex*? That was a present for tonight.

He grinned, and Ky glanced down at him. "What are you thinking about, honey?"

"Christmas. Presents. Moving all the rest of our things over."

"Yeah. That makes me smile too." They were going to do that before the first so his friends could go back to using the condo as a rental. They didn't have a lot—mostly books and toys.

And books.

Also bookcases.

And God, he was so happy to have an office here. No little to no chair space for him anymore. He had an ergonomic wonder.

"Poppy! Daddy! We have to eat so we can open our presents!" Paige beamed at them. "We have to see our bikes!"

He chuckled, and Ky got up, hauling him to his feet. "The little beasts have spoken, honey. Time to eat."

"They taste good!" Henley crowed from the kitchen.

"Hooray, Momma Hen!" Dallas crowed, doing a passable chicken impersonation.

He caught the happy, soft smile on Ky's face, and he was so glad his kid was open and loving and happy to accept this whole co-parenting thing. There was a lot of love in the room right now.

Soon there would be toys and games, a new pair of boots for Kyler, and a framed poster of his last *Maverick* book for Henley.

"You happy, honey?" Ky asked, wrapping an arm around his waist as they walked to the kitchen.

"I am. Next year, we'll have to go see my folks. Henley's welcome to come."

"I'll tell her, but I bet she comes for Thanksgiving and

goes to her momma's for Christmas." Kyler let go to pour them both a cup of joe. "But we'll cross that bridge when we come to it. Dallas wants to introduce me to his granny and grandpa."

"He does. And I imagine they'll come here for Easter now that there's a guest room."

"That's fine, honey. Or they could come in summer when it's so pretty."

"We'll figure it out, I bet." They had...time.

All the time in the world.

"Poppy!" Paige grabbed their hands. "Daddy. Food. Food and then presents!"

They both laughed and nodded, and Henley served up muffins as they got more coffee, and he could hardly bear how good it felt.

He had a new, fascinating family, and he wasn't going it alone anymore, and his body was whispering to him how much Ky wanted him.

Santa had been good to him.

Tonight, Santa was going to be super good to Kyler.

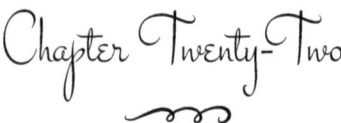

Chapter Twenty-Two

"Daddy!" Paige came running to the car from the school, her pigtails swinging. "*There* you are."

"Here I am." Dallas had gone to a doctor's appointment this afternoon, getting out of school early. His allergies were acting up now that school had been back in session for a few days, so he was picking up Paige and taking her by the coffee place for a hot chocolate. "How's it going?"

"Okay. It was library day, and we played hopscotch in PE. I liked it." She hopped into the back of the truck and got in her car seat. "You?"

"I worked on a saddle all morning, and now here I am to take you to hot choccie." That was Dal's word for it these days.

"Ooh. Perfect. I like that. Are you gay?"

"Huh?" Where had that come from? And so matter of fact, too.

"Eliza at school, she said you were gay. Are you gay?"

He paused, gathering his thoughts. This was important, and he needed to get it right.

"Yeah. I am." There. Bisexual was a little complicated for

her at this age. He and Kayla had discussed that over coffee one afternoon after she'd gone to champion Paige at with the 4-H leaders.

She was a solid friend, and he was discovering that he was beginning to fit in, find his community here.

"Okay..." It took her a second, and then she asked. "What's gay?"

"It means I love your Poppy." That was easy. So easy. "So if a man and a woman are together, they call it straight. But if a man and a man are in love, or a woman and a woman, they call it gay."

"Oh. Okay. So, are we having spaghettis for supper or tacos? Is Dallas going to have to get a shot?"

"I think he probably is, and noodles will be easier on him. That way if he wants his with butter, he can do that." Okay. Just whoosh. God, he loved this kid.

"Oh, then noodles. And a cookie. He needs a cookie. Poor Dal..."

His phone rang, AJ's name coming up. "Hey, honey. How'd he do?"

"He's very brave. He needed a breathing treatment. We're heading home now."

"We're getting a hot chocolate, then we'll head your way."

"Okay, babe."

"Give him a gentle hug for me." Poor baby. "Paige wants to bring him a cookie."

"That's great. He can put that away for later. Nothing milky, though."

"Got it."

"What are we doing for supper, or is tonight the night you're going to play wingman for Kayla?"

He chuckled. "No. That's Thursday. Tonight it's noodles and maybe *Coco* since Dal is feeling so poorly." Disney always did the trick.

"Ah. Right. I don't have the calendar in front of me. I've got sprint club that evening, so it's perfect."

"She's so nervous. Karaoke. Why did I agree to that?" he asked.

"Because you're a good friend. And she's a hoot." AJ chuckled softly. "I should have Ford and Stoney go and take video."

"I will beat you." He wouldn't, but...

"Daddy doesn't beat anyone," Paige called. "He's not vibolent!"

He heard Dallas's soft giggle over the phone.

"You're right, baby girl," AJ said. "Okay, noodles then?"

"Yes, sir. And garlic bread. We have stuff for—"

"No salad, Poppy. Green beans."

"Green beans. We totally have green beans."

He laughed. "Green bings it is."

"Ooooh." That was Paige. "Good call, Dal. Did you know our dads are gay?"

"Uh-huh."

"Why didn't you tell me?" she demanded.

"You didn't ask."

He heard AJ's sharp bark of laughter, and he knew they would be discussing this after supper. They always had so much to talk about with the kids.

"Enjoy your choccie, babe. I'll see you at home. I'll feed the dogs, the chickens, and the cat."

"Thanks, love. I'll do the rest when I get there. Love you."

"Love you too."

"Love you, Daddy! Love you, Paige!"

Paige waved as if they could see her. "Love you, Dal and Poppy!"

He hung up and headed for the coffee shop. He would get something decadent for AJ too. To go.

Kyler was suddenly eager to get home to the rest of his family.

"Can we get choccie in a paper cup, Daddy? Dal had a hard day and I want to see him."

Sounded like his girl felt the same way. That was what he'd hoped for. "Sure, kiddo. We'll get everyone something and head home."

"Cool." She kicked her feet and sang a little song.

Lord, when he'd started building his house in Aspen, he'd had no idea it was going to turn into the place where everything he loved was safe and sound and waiting for him.

Thank God Austin and Dallas had wanted a cowboy for their very own.

Want More?

Interested in learning more about BA's cowboys? Want free fiction and news? Join my newsletter or follow me on Ream!

About BA

Western to the bone and an unrepentant Daddy's Girl, BA Tortuga spends her days with her hounds and her beloved wife, having mother-daughter dates, and eating Mexican food. When she's not doing that, she's writing. She spends her days off watching rodeo, knitting, and surfing Pinterest in the name of research. Following their own personal joys, BA and Julia heard the call of the high desert and they now live in the New Mexico mountains. BA's personal saviors include her wife, her best friends, and coffee. Lots of coffee. Really good coffee.

Having written everything from fist-fighting cowboys to rural single dads to werewolves, BA does her damnedest to tell the stories of her heart, which is committed to giving everyone their happily ever after. With books ranging from heart-warming stories of found families, to rodeo cowboys that are fighting to make a mark, to fiery passionate love affairs, BA refuses to be pigeon-holed by anyone but the voices in her head.

Also Available from BA

Gay Romance

BA's Cozy Cowboys (cowboys w/ kids novels)

Back in the Saddle

Cowboy Haven

Cowboy in the Crosshairs

Cowboy Logic

Cowboy's Law

In the Morning Light

Ranch Manny

Security Detail: an AusTex novel

Silver Buckle Linings

The Cowboy Contract

The Cowboy Guardian

The Cowboy's Texan

The Meaning of Life

Trial by Fire: an AusTex novel

Two Cowboys and a Baby

Two of a Kind

The Banished Series

In Wulf's Clothing

River's Edge

Aspen's Song

The Border Crossing Series

Bombs and Guacamole

Ammo and Enchiladas

The Cereus Series

Cereus: Building

Cereus: Opening

Cereus: Training

Cereus: Rescue

The Cowboy Wanted Series

Cowboy Healing

Second Chance Cowboy

The Foster Ranch Series

The Cowboy Contract

The Cowboy Guardian

The Cowboy's Texan

Leanin' N Ranch Series

Commitment Ranch

Finding Mr. Wright

Whiskey to Wine

Come Back Around

This Old Wind

Perfectly Seasoned

Love is Blind Series

Ever the Same

Real World

Midnight Rodeo Series

Welcome to the Pack

Tails and Whiskers

Above the Fold

Brownie's Sway

Thack's Angel

Here, Kitty Kitty

The Recovery Series

Refired

Slip

The Release Series

The Terms of Release

The Articles of Release

Catch and Release

The Road Trip Series

Racing the Moon • Steam and Sunshine

Under Pressure • Walking on the Sun

Roughstock Series

Blind Ride

And a Smile

File Gumbo

Back to Back

Pulled from All Sides

Coke's Clown

Leading the Blind

The Sanctuary Series
Just Like Cats and Dogs
What the Cat Dragged In

The Spirit Quest Series
Crossing the River
Chasing the Moon
Breaking the Ice

The Stormy Weather Series
Rain and Whiskey
Tropical Depression
Hurricane

Two is Never Enough Series
Claiming Their Mate
Needing to Breathe

Contemporary Standalones
Adding to the Collection
Back Forty
Best New Artist
Boys in the Band
Broken In
Elite Connections
Fighting Addiction
Latigo
Living in Fast Forward

Mud, Movies, Bullets, and Bulls

Needing To

Old Town New

Rainbow Rodeo

Rough in Wranglers

Say Something

Seashores of Old Mexico

Soft Place to Fall

Stetsons and Stakeouts

Truth or Consequences

Wicked in Wranglers

Historical Standalones

Cabin Fever

Hammer and Tongs

Oranges and Peppermints

Paranormal Standalones

Baker's Dozen

Calling His Bluff

Forged in Magic

Long Black Cadillac

Luck of the Draw

Redemption's Ride

Roman and Cage

Setting His Sights

Things that Go Bump in the Night

Unearthed

Wolf Run

Lesbian Romance

Summit Springs Series

Christmas Bizarre w/ Jodi Payne

High Note

Honeymoon in the Cards w/ Jodi Payne

Tipping the Barrel

Contemporary Standalones

Bright Lights and Boobjobs

Games Girls Play

Historical Standalones

Bustles and Doeskins

With Jodi Payne

The Collaborations Series

Refraction

Syncopation

The Cowboy and the Dom Series

First Rodeo

Razor's Edge

No Ghosts

The Soldier and the Angel

The East Meets Westerns Universe

Temptation Ranch

Les's Bar Series

Just Dex

Hide Bound

Wholly Trinity

New Tricks

Merry Everything Series

Window Dressing

Cowboy Protection

Cowboy and Cupcakes

On the Ranch Series

Tending Tyler

Roped In

Diamonds in the Rough

Wrecked Series

Wrecked

Flying Blind

Special Delivery

Seeds and Sunshine

Pick Up Man

The Higher Elevation Series

Land of Enchantment

Keeping Promises

Bigger than Us

Heart of a Cowboy

Home Free

The Sin Deep Series
Sin Deep
The Trouble with Cowboys

The Triskelion Series
Breaking the Rules
Making a Mark
Making the Rules

Hey, y'all!

Thank you for giving Covering the Cowboy a try. I hope you enjoyed the story, and will consider leaving a review at the eBook retailer website where you made your purchase.

Don't forget to "like" my BA Tortuga page on Facebook to keep up with new releases, author news, special discount codes and sale announcements. And if you're interested in sneak peeks, rodeo pictures, and general fun, please come see the BA's Cowboys on Facebook. We'd love to have all y'all!

Yeehaw!

BA

Milton Keynes UK
Ingram Content Group UK Ltd.
UKHW030148051224
452010UK00001B/43